ROSIE'S TEXAS FAMILY

A Rosie's Family Mystery

BY

SUZANNE FLOYD

COPYRIGHT

This is a work of fiction. All characters in this book have no existence outside the imagination of the author. The town of Promise is a composite of many small towns anywhere.

Copyright January 2021 by Suzanne Floyd. All rights reserved. No part of this book may be reproduced in any form, save for inclusion of brief quotations in a review, without the written permission of the author. www.SuzanneFloyd.com

Cover by Bella Media Management

I dedicate this book to my husband Paul and our daughters, Camala and Shannon, and all my family. Thanks for all your support and encouragement.

"Once Lost, now found. Eternally thankful!" Our Daily Bread

PROLOGUE

"What time will you be over for Thanksgiving dinner on Thursday?" Jacob Fallon stood in the doorway between his office and that of his great-grandson. He put on a good face as he looked at Jeremy.

"I've told you several times that I'm leaving for Texas in the morning. I'm taking some time off. I'm not sure how long I'll be gone," he added. He didn't know if his great-grandfather was getting forgetful, or was simply being stubborn. If he thought he could wear Jeremy down on this subject, he was going to be disappointed.

"What do you mean you don't know how long you'll be gone? This started as a couple of days for Christmas. Now you're talking about longer. You can't take off indefinitely."

"So fire me." Jeremy was tired of being told what he could and couldn't do. He had let it go on far too long already. It was time to take a stand.

"Are you daring me?" The older man's eyes narrowed. He didn't know what to make of Jeremy's new attitude. Since returning from their trip to Iowa during the summer, something had changed.

"No, I'm not daring you." Jeremy turned to face his great-grandfather. "I'm saying I need some time to figure a few things out."

"Like what?" Jacob frowned at him. Suspicion darkened his faded eyes.

In the past six months, Jeremy had started questioning things he'd been told all of his life. He'd known for a long time that he wasn't cut out to run the company Jacob had inherited from his uncle more than sixty years ago. Making his great-grandfather accept that was another matter. The old man wouldn't listen.

"Like what I want to do with my life." He held up his hand to stop the older man from interrupting. "I've tried to tell you

I'm not cut out to run the company, but you refuse to listen. I've also told you I have some ideas that would be good for the company and help it grow. You won't listen to that either. Maybe it's time I took those ideas elsewhere." He'd never spoken to his great-grandfather in this manner before. That was the problem. If he'd been more assertive in the past, he might not be facing this dilemma now.

Jacob took a step back, his mouth slack for a few seconds. "You would work for one of our competitors?"

"Not by choice, but if you won't listen to anything I have to say, you leave me no other option. You expect me to run this company, but you won't let me make any decisions."

"This company has been owned and operated by Fallons for more than a hundred and fifty years. There is value in tradition." Once again he wasn't listening to what Jeremy was saying.

Jeremy shrugged. "There is also value in being able to make your own choices in life."

The older man shook his head. "I suppose this has something to do with *those people* in Iowa. They fed you a lot of nonsense about something that happened long before you were born." His voice was harsh when he mentioned Shep and Parker Baker.

"*Those people* are Shep and Parker, and they didn't say anything about what happened back then. Even if you and great-grandmother hadn't gone to Iowa, I would still be feeling the way I do right now. I don't want to be CEO of this company or any other. That's not what I'm cut out for."

Since meeting Shep and Parker Baker this past summer, he and Shep had talked several times. The initial invitation to visit his Texas family for Christmas had been extended to Thanksgiving through New Year's. Maybe he'd find what he was looking for.

"Would you rather the company I've spent my entire life building up for my heirs was turned over to a bunch of strangers?"

"Frankly, I don't care who you turn the company over to as long as it isn't me. The person who should succeed you is Kenneth. Other than you, he knows more about the running of Fallon Industries than anyone."

"He isn't family," Jacob scoffed.

"Yes, he is, just not the right family in your view. I don't know why he puts up with the way you treat him. I don't understand why Great-grandmother tolerates you treating Kenneth the way you do either. He's her great-nephew after all."

"*Her* great-nephew," Jacob emphasized, "not mine. That's the difference. This company belongs to Fallons. It always has and it always will. That means you. You're the last remaining Fallon."

"So you keep reminding me. That doesn't mean I'm cut out for the job. What do you think would happen to the company if my heart wasn't in running it?" Jeremy was digging in his heels.

Jeremy had never thought to question how his great-grandfather had come to inherit the company that should have gone to his cousin. After this long, there were few people left in town that remembered any details about what happened more than sixty years ago.

Gossips might have speculated at the time about how convenient it was for Jacob that his uncle had a stroke right then. But there wasn't even that now. Jeremy didn't want to believe his great-grandfather would kill someone for any reason. But Jacob was ruthless when it came to business.

He'd done some digging in old copies of the local newspaper without learning much there either. The most anyone had done at the time was to advertise in several large newspapers hoping Barnard would learn of his father's death. In any case, Barnard had never been heard from again.

"Jeremy, you're being unreasonable." Jacob's voice broke in on Jeremy's thoughts. "I simply can't let you take an extended amount of time off. You're needed here."

"No, I'm not. I guess the only choice you're left with then is to fire me because I'm taking this time."

"You're family, I can't fire you."

Jeremy lifted his shoulders in a shrug. "Then I'll see you after the first of the year."

"That's more than a month from now." The more Jacob argued the more determined Jeremy was. This was unacceptable but he didn't know what to do. He'd never seen this side of his great-grandson, and didn't know how to combat it. "It's bad enough that you won't be here for Thanksgiving, but how am I to tell your great-grandmother that you won't be with us for Christmas either?"

"She has been aware that I was going to Texas for Christmas since the summer. I'll call to wish you both a Merry Christmas and Happy New Year." They had been discussing his upcoming trip since they returned from Iowa. By now, they should understand he wasn't going to change his mind.

"The company will come to a standstill with you gone for this length of time," Jacob continued to press.

"I seriously doubt that. You would never let that happen. Besides, Kenneth can do his job and mine with one hand tied behind his back. As I've said on several occasions, Kenneth is a natural when it comes to business. I'm not."

Jacob huffed, but didn't comment. No one argued with him and won, but it looked like this was going to be a first. He'd never realized how stubborn Jeremy was. The more he argued his point, the more Jeremy refused to listen to reason. Maybe it was time for Kenneth to find other employment. If Kenneth wasn't around for Jeremy to rely on to take up the slack, he might finally accept the inevitable.

"I'll stop by for dinner tonight," Jeremy said. "I want to see great-grandmother before I leave."

"Having you gone over the holidays will break her heart." If reason didn't work, maybe guilt would.

"She'll get over it." Jeremy picked up his laptop case. "I've already briefed Kenneth on everything I've been working on. It will be a seamless transition." He held out his hand to his great-grandfather. "I'll see you at six this evening."

"What do you mean transition? You are coming back." It sounded like an order. Jeremy had already left the office and didn't answer.

Walking out of the building, he felt like a heavy weight had been lifted off his shoulders. He had to deal with one more confrontation before this subject was done. It might even be worse than the one he'd just survived. Victoria was very good at laying on the guilt. But this was something he had to do for himself. If they couldn't, or wouldn't, accept that... He shrugged. He wasn't going to change his mind.

CHAPTER ONE

Walking down the jetway at the airport, a flutter of nerves attacked Jeremy's stomach. Was it a mistake coming here? Was Jacob right, and Shep's family was out to take over Fallon Industries? Did they even have any legal claim to the company? He had liked Shep and Parker, but what did he know about them? They had been friendly when he met them during the summer. But he'd only seen them a couple of times. That wasn't long enough to know what they were really like.

Dinner the night before had been grueling. Victoria wasn't any happier than Jacob about his upcoming trip to Texas. She had tried every trick in her arsenal to get him to come around to her way of thinking. There had been a lot of pleading, whining, and heavy doses of guilt. When none of that worked, there were even a few crocodile tears, all to no avail. Her parting words still rang in his ears. "Don't leave us alone in our old age. You are all we have left."

Jeremy tried putting those thoughts aside as he made his way through the airport to the car rental kiosk. He was determined to keep an open mind about the Baker family. Not everyone had ulterior motives behind everything they did.

The closest large airport to the ranch was more than an hour away. Instead of having someone pick him up, he had decided to rent a car. Besides, it was a good idea to have his own transportation in case things didn't work out with Shep's parents and grandparents.

What if Shep's grandfather tried to claim Fallon Industries for himself? He knew that was what Jacob was afraid of. Did he even have any right to the company? Once again the doubts that his great-grandparents had tried putting in his mind assailed him. It would be different if the senior Baker had been raised by his father and mother. But that wasn't the case.

When Barnard Fallon came home from the war he found that his fiancé had married someone else while he was gone.

That someone was his cousin Jacob. Barnard's father had wanted him to take over the business, but Barnard didn't want to be stuck behind a desk. Instead, he left Kansas and no one had seen or heard from him again.

Within a month his father had a massive stroke and died. The company should have gone to Barnard, but no one knew where he was, or if he was even alive. There weren't the tools back then to locate people that were available today, but no one had tried to find Barnard either. Since there were no other heirs, Jacob had taken over Fallon Industries. He'd been at the helm ever since.

The family history was still somewhat of a mystery to Jeremy. His great-grandparents didn't talk about the past. He did know that Shep's grandfather was the son of Jacob's cousin, Barnard.

It was only after the true identity of the famous author, RS. Fallon was discovered that anyone knew there had indeed been another heir. Rosie Shepard had a baby out of wedlock. She had chosen that pen name to honor the man she had loved, Barnard Fallon. He hadn't lived long enough to see his son.

It would crush Jacob to lose something he'd spent more than sixty years building. No matter how Jacob came to inherit the company from his uncle, he had worked hard to make it what it was today. He wouldn't turn the company over without a fight.

Maybe this hadn't been such a smart move, Jeremy thought. He shook his head. Second-guessing his decision now wasn't going to do any good. He would go with the flow and see what happened.

There were going to be a lot of people at the ranch during the holidays. Parker's family was coming from Arizona right after Thanksgiving. Maybe he should have waited until there wouldn't be such a large crowd. Because his grandparents had both died before he was born and his parents hadn't been a part of his life since he was a young boy, holiday dinners consisted of him and his great-grandparents. He wasn't afraid of large crowds, but it might get a little overwhelming.

Leaving the airport behind, the open range stretched out in front of him. Even in college, he'd lived in the city. Until he'd followed his great-grandparents to Iowa this last summer, he'd never been out of Kansas. He loved the openness here. You're not in Kansas anymore, Toto, he silently quoted a line from *The Wizard of Oz*.

After Shep had invited him to spend the holidays with his family in Texas, he'd researched the area. Cattle ranching and oil were what Texas was known for, but Texas was a big state. There were a lot of other things to see and do here.

Before committing to any longer than Christmas, he'd wait and see how things went. He wanted to see as much as he could before returning to the snow and cold of Kansas. At some point, he was going to have to force Jacob to listen to him. Either that or simply walk away from that life, the way Barnard and Jeremy's dad had done. Could he do that to the only people in his life that had always been there for him? He didn't know the answer to that question.

He only knew that he had been feeling boxed in even before graduating from college the year before. It had been an accepted fact that he would eventually take over the running of Fallon Industries from Jacob. But he knew that wasn't what he wanted. He wasn't cut out to be the CEO of any company. Simply thinking of it caused his chest to constrict.

What he'd said to Jacob was true. He needed time to decide what he wanted to do with his life, to find where he fit in. Although Jacob had been grooming him to take over the company since he was big enough to sit behind a desk, he knew that wasn't what he wanted to do with his life. Convincing Jacob of that was the problem. He turned a deaf ear to anything Jeremy said.

Following the older couple to Iowa, that summer had proven to his great-grandfather that he wasn't just a puppet to be manipulated into doing whatever the older man wanted. It had also given him the chance to see other opportunities and choices. He wanted to explore those opportunities.

Driving aimlessly, he took in the scenery. There was a lot of open space everywhere he looked. His stomach growled reminding him he'd only had a light breakfast before going to the airport in Kansas City. He'd always heard that farmers and ranchers ate their big meal at noon having a light meal in the evening. If that was the case here, he'd need something now to get him through until morning. There was still plenty of time before he was due at the Baker ranch He didn't want to get there too soon and throw off their timetable.

Punctuality was something else Great-grandfather had drilled into him. If you weren't five minutes early, you were late. But being several hours early wasn't polite either. He'd only given Shep an approximate time when he would arrive, but even so, arriving hours earlier than he was expected wouldn't make a good first impression.

Turning his thoughts to food, he headed for the small town of Promise, Texas. It was one of the many small, quirky towns that dotted the landscape. Parking in front of a small diner, a lopsided grin tilted his lips upward. The town reminded him of old westerns he enjoyed watching on TV.

Pushing open the car door, he drew in a deep breath of the fresh air. The mild temperature was a welcome change from what he'd left behind. Snow was two feet deep in some places at home. This was something he could get used to.

His stomach growled again reminding him why he'd stopped. Pushing open the door of the small diner, the aroma of fresh coffee and fried chicken greeted him along with a broad smile from the waitress.

"Howdy, Darlin'. Welcome to The Cowtown Café."

He looked over his shoulder to see if she was talking to someone else. Nope. No one came in behind him. She was talking to him. "Um, hello?" He'd always heard of Southern hospitality, but this was the first time he experienced it. The woman reminded him of Mary Lou at A-Cup-A-Joe in Whitehaven, Iowa.

"Grab a seat anywhere," the waitress said. "We don't stand of formalities 'round here." Jeremy judged her to be somewhere in her forties. Her brown hair was pulled up in a ponytail to keep it off her face while she bustled around. Instead of sitting at one of the few unoccupied tables, he sat down at the counter. Even though it was past noon, the diner was busy. Taking up a table for one person didn't seem right.

"I'm Erma Jean." The woman placed a glass of water on the counter in front of him. She studied him for a minute. "I'll bet you're that cousin the Bakers are lookin' forward to havin' visit." She smiled at him.

Surprise registered on his handsome face. "Um, yes, I'm Jeremy Fallon." He automatically reached out to shake her hand. "How did you know?" He could feel people watching him at her pronouncement.

"Why, Darlin', this here is a small town. Everybody knows everybody else's business. Yer all Dan and Mona have been talkin' 'bout for the past month." She chuckled. "Besides, there's no denyin' the family resemblance. You look just like the rest of the Baker boys. You want coffee while you decide what you want to eat? I just made a fresh pot. The special of the day is fried chicken, mashed taters, and gravy with mixed vegetables." She placed a menu beside the glass of water.

"Coffee would be fine. Thank you. That special sounds pretty good. I'll have that."

She was back quickly, placing a heavy mug in front of him. "The whole Baker clan has been lookin' forward to your visit," she picked up the conversation where she'd left off. "Hope you're plannin' on stickin' 'round longer than a few days. Shep and Parker just pulled in a couple days ago. It's gonna be a big Thanksgiving and Christmas for everyone."

He couldn't decide whether she was being nosy or just friendly. He wasn't used to people knowing his personal business. He decided to go with friendly. "I'm not sure how long I'll be here." It all depended on what the reception at the ranch was like, he amended. If what she said was true, this might turn out to be as good as he was hoping. Even though he was distantly related to the Bakers, he couldn't call them family.

"Well, welcome to Promise. I hope y'all enjoy yer visit. Lots doin' in these parts at this time of year. The whole week before Christmas we have a big festival here in town. Hope y'all will stick around long 'nuf to join in." She winked at him as she turned away, placing his order on the wheel above the pass-through window to the kitchen.

He kept looking around to see who else she was talking to, but it was only him. Y'all must mean one person instead of a group of people, he decided. How would she describe a group of people? He chuckled to himself.

It didn't take long for her to come back with a plate so full gravy dripped over the side. Even as hungry as he was, he didn't know if he could eat that much. Taking leftovers to the ranch didn't sound like the polite thing to do either.

He didn't need to worry about leftovers though. After the first bite of chicken, he barely stopped long enough to take a breath. "That was delicious," he told Erma Jean when she picked up his empty plate. "I don't recall the last time I've had fried chicken that good." His great-grandparents had a cook, but she didn't make anything this tasty.

The constant inspection from the other people in the diner was beginning to make him uncomfortable. A man at the end of the counter barely took his eyes off him. "You have a good day now, Bill," Erma Jean said as she placed his tab on the counter in front of him. His answer to her comment was an unintelligible grunt. Erma Jean didn't seem to notice. Maybe he was always that surly.

Tossing several bills down beside his plate, the man stood up. With a final glare in Jeremy's direction, he left letting the door slam in his wake. Jeremy dismissed the man. He had enough other things on his mind to worry about. One rude person didn't matter.

Back outside, he groaned softly. He was stuffed. If he ate like this every day, he'd need to run ten miles instead of the five miles he currently ran each morning. There wouldn't be enough hours of daylight for all of that plus the hours he spent working at Fallon Industries. Just thinking about it made him tired.

He sighed. He'd led a sheltered life as well as a soft life. That was only part of what was bothering him. Instead of spending all of his time behind a desk, he needed to be doing something physical. The time he spent in the gym didn't count. With another sigh, he headed to his rental car. The restlessness that had plagued him in the past year reared its ugly head. Being cooped up in an office was looking less and less appealing every day.

Lost in those thoughts, he almost ran into the man who had been staring at him in the diner. Standing in the middle of the sidewalk, he didn't bother to step aside to let Jeremy pass.

"Yer name Fallon?" His voice was a low growl.

"Yes?" It came out sounding more like a question. He tried to step around the man.

"Not so fast." He put his hand on Jeremy's chest to stop him from moving. "Yer old man is a real prick."

Jeremy was taken aback for a second. How did this man know his father? "Thank you for your opinion. Now if you'll excuse me." His first impression of the small southern town had been how friendly people were. Now he was getting a different impression. Again, Jeremy tried to move around the man. He had no idea who he was or how he knew his dad. Davis might not be much of a father, but that didn't have anything to do with Jeremy.

"I said the man's a prick."

"Yes, I heard you." Jeremy wasn't going to let a stranger goad him into an argument. He even agreed with the man. Davis preferred spending his time on some artistic endeavor somewhere other than with his son. Jeremy saw him so rarely that he barely knew his own father.

"Aren't you gonna say anything?"

"No."

"He ruined my life."

"I'm sorry to hear that, but that doesn't have anything to do with me."

"Tell him I said payback's a bitch."

"I'll do that the next time I see him if you'll give me your name." The man didn't bother answering as he marched off.

Jeremy stared at the man's back with his mouth hanging open. What was that about? He had no idea who the man was. Davis spent very little time in the United States. How had he ruined the man's life?

In his twenty-two years, he'd probably spent less than five years total with his dad. He was sure Davis was afraid Jacob would put him to work if he spent more time than that in Kansas. Whatever that man had against Davis had nothing to do with Jeremy. He wasn't going to spend a lot of time worrying about it. Dismissing the encounter, he unlocked the door of his rental car.

It was still too early to show up at the Baker ranch. Outside of town, he took a side road. Fences lined the road keeping cattle and horses inside. With all this open space and a brisk wind, his idea of a wind farm would be feasible. In fact, there were several wind farms already in operation in Texas. But he hadn't seen any since he left the airport.

Manufacturing the parts necessary for the windmills would add to the production of Fallon Industries. Unfortunately, Jacob wasn't interested. The only ideas he cared about were his own.

How did he figure anyone would be able to run the company if he wouldn't let them lead? He gave a frustrated sigh. That was one of the many reasons Jeremy wasn't interested in taking over as CEO. Jacob would always second-guess anything he did.

When a large house appeared at the top of a small rise, he pulled over. Another house could be seen in the distance. This one was in the process of being built. They looked out of place among all the cattle and horses he'd seen grazing in the fields. The field surrounding the fancy house had no horses or cattle to spoil the view from the top of the hill. He was willing to bet a real rancher didn't live there. What would someone with a big house like that think of a windmill in their back yard? They probably wouldn't like it.

He'd heard some of the arguments against wind energy: they spoiled the view, they killed birds, the infrastructure to get a wind farm up and running was too expensive. Those were only some of the arguments. He sighed. People with that mindset were a great deal like Jacob, so set in their ways that they couldn't see a different future than what was already here.

What would Shep's family think if he proposed having a windmill to produce the energy for their house? The farm where Shep and Parker lived would also be an ideal for a windmill. There was plenty of open space and there was enough wind to make it profitable.

After his visit during the summer, he'd researched the Baker family. They were a close-knit group in spite of the fact that two of Shep's brothers no longer lived in Promise. The elder Barker's adoptive parents had owned hundreds of acres of land. They'd gotten in on the oil boom early enough to take in large profits. The older couple still lived on that ranch. Shep's parents also owned a large ranch and his father was a veterinarian.

He chuckled softly. Great-grandfather didn't have to worry that the Bakers were after his money. They could probably buy and sell him several times over.

None of that gave Jacob any comfort. The saying "the more money someone has, the more they want,' certainly applied to him.

It didn't look like Shep and Parker were in dire need of money either. Parker had inherited a sizeable estate from her great-aunt, who happened to be Shep's great-grandmother.

They also received income from all the books that R.S. Fallon had written. After the story came out about the woman's life, there had been a resurgence of interest in her books. Most of them were back on the best seller's list.

He hadn't been able to learn much online about the rest of Parker's family. Her adoptive father was a psychologist. Her mother worked in an office. Parker's twin brothers were in their second year of college. From what little he had learned about the Evans family, it appeared they were also close. Where had his family gone wrong?

He had tried to explain all of this to Jacob, but he wasn't interested in listening. He was the sort to think everyone was out to get what he had. Lately, Jeremy had considered the possibility that Jacob was projecting his desires onto those around him. If that was the case, had Jacob helped his uncle toward having a stroke?

Was something like that even possible, especially sixty years ago? He didn't know enough about medicine to figure that out. Besides, if Jacob had done something like that, he didn't want to know.

Kansas had a fair number of millionaires, but he wasn't sure if his great-grandfather qualified for that title. The one time he'd asked about his financial standing, he'd been told that until he took over as head of Fallon Industries that was none of his business.

How does he expect me to assume control of the company if I don't know the financial side of it? he asked himself. He probably expects to live forever. The snarky thought came out of nowhere. It was fine with him if Jacob continued to run the company for the next fifty years as long as he could do his own thing.

Even the few hours he'd been away from the company and his great-grandfather's influence, he felt lighter than he had in years. Jacob called all the shots without giving any thought to what he or his great-grandmother wanted. That only served to enforce what he already knew. He wasn't the person to take over when Jacob finally retired. Convincing him of that wouldn't be easy though. Giving a weary sigh, he shook his head. Jacob would never agree unless he could show that he would better serve Fallon Industries in a different capacity.

For a long while, he stared at the countryside without seeing it. His mind was lost somewhere else. Jacob and Victoria had raised him when his parents divorced. Jacob called Davis a dreamer like Barnard had been. He preferred to concentrate on his art rather than run a business. His mother hadn't wanted to be tied down with a small child and willingly signed custody over to Jacob and Victoria. At least that was the story he had been raised with. He seldom saw either of his parents.

Jeremy wasn't a dreamer like his father. But business didn't consume him the way it did his great-grandfather. He wanted something more out of life than either of them had. He couldn't say exactly what that was though.

How would things have been different if Barnard had lived long enough to marry Rosie and raise their son? Where would that have left him? Would Jacob still have inherited the company when his uncle passed on? Barnard hadn't wanted the company when he returned from the war. Would he have changed his mind once he had a family to support?

He didn't know enough about Barnard to even guess at the answer. Until it had been made public that the author R.S. Fallon had a child out of wedlock by Barnard Fallon, no one had thought much about how Jacob had come to inherit Fallon Industries. Even though there weren't the resources there were now to locate missing people someone couldn't simply disappear without leaving some sort of a trail. It didn't appear that anyone had tried very hard to find him. He had a lot of questions without any answers.

Was this part of the reason he was feeling so restless? He shook his head. The restlessness had started before he knew anything about Barnard. Would he find what he was looking for in Texas?

He shook his head to clear these thoughts. It was useless asking all the 'what if' questions. The past was just that, the past. There was no way to change things now.

Checking the clock on the dashboard, he was surprised at the time. He'd been sitting alongside the road longer than he realized. It was time to go to the Baker ranch. Another case of jittery nerves settled in his stomach.

For the first time in a very long time, he whispered a prayer that everything would be okay. His great-grandparents weren't much for going to church. He hoped there was a God, and He had put this family in his life for a reason. Drawing a calming breath, he pulled back onto the road heading for the unknown.

CHAPTER TWO

"Why don't you go out and check on the horses with Shep," Lena Baker suggested. Her husband had been pacing the length of the porch for the past hour. "It might take your mind off this young man's visit." He didn't want to admit he was nervous about meeting Jeremy, but he couldn't hide that fact from his wife of close to fifty years.

Placing a kiss on her cheek, he sighed. "Don't know why meetin' this young man has me tied up in knots," he reluctantly admitted. "It'll be no different than meetin' any other stranger."

Lena chuckled. "But he's not just another stranger, he's blood kin."

"There is that," he said with another sigh. "I was content not knowin' about my birth folks. This has stirred up a whole lot of questions."

"Answers can't hurt you," she said. "Shep and Parker said Jeremy was nice when they met him. You need to relax. He won't bite any of us."

"You always know what to say when I get all het up over somethin'. I'll go see if Shep needs some help with the horses." Chuckling, he kissed her cheek again before heading down the steps.

As Lena knew would happen, working with the horses calmed her husband's nerves right down. There was something about animals that could work wonders on a body's nerves. By the time Jeremy turned his rental car into the long drive, Ralph was ready to meet him.

Jeremy stopped before driving up to the house. It was big, but not nearly as big as the mansion he's seen earlier. *Nothing showy here,* he thought. This was a working ranch, not something to show off to their friends. The big barn was about a hundred yards from the house. *Probably to keep the odor of horse and cow manure and the flies from infecting the house,* he thought. He could see several horses in the pasture beyond the barn. A steady wind fluttered the leaves on the big trees shading the house.

This would be an ideal place for a wind turbine. Depending on the size, it could produce enough electricity to run the house and all the outbuildings. He dismissed the thought. He wasn't here to talk business. If the opportunity presented itself, he might make a suggestion though. He chuckled. If he could convince enough people to buy the turbines, he just might be able to persuade Jacob that it was a viable idea for Fallon Industries.

As he pulled up to the porch he could see someone sitting on the swing. The bright red color of her hair told him it was Parker. He didn't know either Parker or Shep well enough to be able to pick them out of a crowd, but that hair was enough to identify her.

A frown drew his brows together when she didn't get up to greet him. The look on her face wasn't exactly welcoming. It wasn't unwelcoming either. More curious than anything else, he decided. But why? It wasn't that long since they were together in Iowa. She had been friendly then. Had something happened to change her mind about his visit? Maybe he shouldn't have come here.

~~~

Shep's sister Bailey was sitting on the porch when the strange car pulled into the lane. For several long moments, the car didn't come close to the house. *What's he waiting for? Is he inspecting us? Do we meet his expectations?* Butterflies fluttered in her stomach.

Why was he here? Did he have an ulterior motive? Shep thought he was looking for a family. But was there another reason? She couldn't think of any. Since all the to-do over R.S. Fallon had come out, strange things had been happening. Was he part of that? She hated the fact that she had become suspicious of people's motives.

She wanted Jeremy to like her granddad. He might put on

a tough exterior, but inside was a marshmallow. It would hurt his feelings if Jeremy turned out to be as awful as Shep said his great-granddad was. She couldn't think of anything her granddad had that Jeremy would want. Nothing in Texas belonged to the Fallon family. No one here wanted anything that belonged to him or his great-grandparents either.

Jeremy finally put the car in gear, coasting slowly up to the porch. It was a long moment before he opened the car door. Why didn't he get out? What was he waiting for? With the late afternoon sun glaring on the windshield, she couldn't see who was sitting inside. What if he brought his awful great-granddad with him? Her stomach churned at the thought.

Finally opening the car door, he placed one long leg on the ground and stood up. Even with the dark sunglasses covering his eyes she could feel his gaze on her. He still hadn't said anything.

From her perch on the swing, he seemed tall like Shep. His hair was also dark like Shep's. There really was something about familial traits being passed down through the generations. It didn't matter how distant the relationship was, those traits still showed up.

He didn't move away from the car. Instead, he continued to stare at her, a slight frown wrinkling his forehead. What was he thinking when he looked at her? The heavy silence weighed on her. He finally stepped away from the car, allowing the door to shut.

She breathed a sigh of relief when the rest of the family joined her on the porch. "Howdy, Jeremy. Welcome." Shep stepped off the porch with his hand outstretched in welcome. "It's good to see you again. Come meet the rest of the clan."

Bailey's breath caught in her throat when he took off the dark glasses. The resemblance to Shep was undeniable, but there was something else she couldn't name. Shep was ruggedly handsome, but Jeremy's features were softer, more refined. And definitely handsome, she added.

When Shep introduced Bailey, Jeremy chuckled causing

her to bristle. This was a new experience for her. No one had ever laughed when they met her. She looked down to make sure all her buttons were buttoned and her jeans were zipped. Everything was as it should be. So why did he laugh at her? An angry retort was on the tip of her tongue when he explained.

"When I saw you sitting on the swing, I thought you were Parker. You look enough like her to be her sister. I thought maybe I'd made a mistake coming here when you just sat there."

Bailey released the breath she'd been holding. It was a logical conclusion. Since Parker became part of the family, more than one person had remarked on how much they looked alike.

Jeremy looked around a confused frown on his face. "Parker is here, isn't she?" He'd been under the impression that she and Shep were madly in love. Why would she stay behind if that was true?

"She went upstairs to freshen up a few minutes ago," Shep said. "She'll be right down."

As though she'd heard them talking about her Parker pushed open the door. "I thought I heard people out here. Welcome, Jeremy." She came down the porch steps to give him a brief hug. "It's good to see you again. How was your flight?"

"It's good to see you, too." His eyebrows went up as he took in the small baby bump under her shirt. "You're pregnant." A warm smile lit up his face.

"I'm what?" she teased, causing him to blush. She placed her hand on her rounded tummy. "Yes, I'm pregnant."

"Sorry, I didn't mean to blurt it out like that. I don't know why it surprised me either. I'm happy for you." He placed a kiss on her cheek and offered his hand to Shep.

Gus, Parker's companion and guard dog, whined his displeasure about being ignored. "Well, hello there, Gus." Jeremy bent down to give Gus a good ear rub. "I wasn't sure you'd remember me." He looked up at Parker.

"Oh, he has a long memory for his friends," she assured him.

"And an even longer memory for his enemies," Shep laughed.

"Let's go inside, and Shep can show you where you'll be stayin'," Dan suggested once all the greetings were over. "The breeze is kickin' up some and it's gettin' a little chilly to be standing out here on the porch."

"Chilly?" Jeremy laughed. "I was thinking it was rather warm. It's going to be a long, cold winter in Kansas." Thinking about the weather he left behind, he shivered. *He could get used to this*, he thought again.

"Then you're goin' to enjoy our weather here," Dan said, giving him a friendly pat on the shoulder. "You're welcome to stay as long as you like."

"Does the wind always blow like this?"

"No," Dan answered with a chuckle. "Sometimes the wind really kicks up." That brought a laugh from the others.

"Really. Hmm," was Jeremy's only response. The thought he'd had as he pulled into the lane was beginning to grow in his mind. He'd seen several areas with windmills, but there hadn't been any individual wind turbines at any of the homes he'd seen.

"When was the last time you ate?" Mona asked once they were seated in the great room. "Did they even feed you on the flight?" A fire crackled merrily in the big stone fireplace.

Jeremy gave another laugh. "A small bag of pretzels and a soft drink is all they offer on short flights anymore. I took an early flight so I could do some sightseeing before coming out to the ranch. When I got into Promise, I stopped at a little café."

He looked at Shep and Parker. "It sort of reminded me of that diner in Whitehaven. I guess all small towns have a signature café where all the locals gather. The waitress even put me in mind of Mary Lou. She kept calling me Darlin' and talking about y'all. I kept thinking there were people behind me." He shook his head. "I know that's southern-speak for you, but I kept looking over my shoulder to make sure she wasn't talking to more than me."

Laughing, Dan said, "Y'all means one person, all y'all is two or more." Everyone laughed. "Erma Jean calls everyone Darlin'. It saves her from having to remember names when tourists pass through. She's great with putting faces and food together though. Next time you visit, she'll remember what you ordered today."

"I hope you left room for supper," Mona said. "We've got a roast in the oven with potatoes and carrots. Grams made apple dumplings for dessert."

Jeremy groaned. "You people must be trying to fatten me up. The plate of fried chicken and mashed potatoes was enough to feed a family of four."

"Did you bring any pictures of Barnard with you?" Tired of talking about food, Ralph spoke up. The one picture Parker and Shep had found of Barnard, he had been only a few years older than Jeremy was now. He could see the family resemblance in this young man.

Jeremy nodded his dark head. "My great-grandfather didn't have many, but I was able to find several in some old photo albums belonging to my great-grandmother. I can get them out of my suitcase now if you'd like." He started to stand up.

"Time enough for that later," Ralph said, holding up his hand. "I never thought much about my birth family until Parker and Shep discovered Rosie's journals. She didn't know much about Barnard though. I thought it might be interestin' to know a little more about the family's roots."

"I'm not going to be able to fill in many blanks," Jeremy said. "He was gone long before I was born. My great-grandparents aren't the sentimental sort, so they never spoke about the past while I was growing up. Most of what I heard was from others in town or old copies of the newspaper. After it was revealed who R.S. Fallon was and that she'd had Barnard's baby, there was plenty of gossip."

There was also gossip about how Barnard's father had conveniently died shortly after Barnard left town. The only remaining heir had been Jacob. He had taken over Fallon Industries. He didn't want to think about what some of the people were hinting at.

"As you can guess, there aren't many people left in town who remember Barnard. After last summer, I started asking some questions. I pressed Victoria until she finally gave me an old photo album. That's where I found the few pictures I have." He gave a small laugh. "As you can imagine, that didn't make Jacob very happy. I'll be happy to tell you what little I learned about Barnard though."

Bailey was fascinated with this new relative. "Did your great-grandparents raise you?" she asked. The past was important, but she wanted to know about him, not his ancestors.

Nodding his head, a lock of dark hair fell onto his forehead. In an automatic gesture, he tossed his head to put it back in place. A small grin tugged at her lips. She'd seen each of her brothers do the same thing thousands of times.

It was fascinating to see how men from different backgrounds could be so much alike because they shared some of the same genes. It wasn't just his looks either. Their facial expressions and gestures were so similar it was shocking.

"As far back as I can remember I've lived with Victoria and Jacob. I never knew my grandparents and my parents are divorced. My dad prefers art to people. Great-grandfather says my father is a dreamer like Barnard." A lopsided grin lifted one side of his mouth. "He calls it a recessive gene that has been passed down from Barnard's side of the family. He's tried his best to weed that gene out of me. So far, he's only been half successful."

"Do you have any siblings?" Shaking his head, that same lock of hair fell forward. Bailey's fingers itched with the desire to run her fingers through his thick hair. She sat on her hands to prevent that from happening.

After dinner or supper as it was called in Texas, Jeremy showed them the pictures he'd managed to find of Barnard. Seeing the one of him in his Army uniform, Mona drew in a sharp breath. Standing up, she went to the fireplace mantle and took down a picture. Handing it to Jeremy, his mouth dropped open. It was Shep when he was in the Army, but it could be Barnard in a different uniform. The similarities between the two men were uncanny.

It was late when Ralph and Lena headed home. Jeremy hadn't been able to tell them as much as he'd hoped, but he was satisfied with what he'd learned. What Rosie had said in her journals about the man she had loved for the remainder of her life was enough for him. Barnard had been a nice man. It appeared that Shep and Parker were right about Jeremy as well. He was more like Barnard than his great-grandfather.

He was sure Jeremy's great-grandfather could tell him more about Barnard since they'd been first cousins and of the same generation. But he didn't want to know bad enough to meet the older Fallon. From what little Shep and Parker had said about him, he was more interested in his company than people.

If Jacob Fallon was worried about losing his precious company to the Bakers, Ralph would gladly set his mind to rest. Family was more important to Ralph than any company. The old man could keep it. He hoped it gave him comfort in his old age.

Barnard had cared deeply for Rosie, and he would have been a good father to their son. It was hard for him to think of himself in that manner. He was the son of Rhoda and Willard Baker, not Rosie Shepard and Barnard Fallon. He was more interested in getting to know Jeremy, instead of Barnard.

"Shep and Parker were right about Jeremy," Lena said, interrupting her husband's musings. "He seems like a nice young man. No matter what kind of people his great-grandparents are, he turned out okay."

"I think you're right." Reaching out for his wife's hand, Ralph looked at her in the greenish glow from the dashboard. "I think there's a bit of Barnard living in each of his descendants, including Jeremy."

"You didn't even ask what kind of company Jeremy's great-grandfather owns," Lena pointed out. "I thought you might be interested in learning something about it."

Ralph shrugged in the dark. "It might be interesting to learn what kind of business Barnard's father started, but there's plenty of time for that later. Everything I could want is right here." He brought her hand up to place a kiss on the back. "I wouldn't mind knowin' why Barnard walked away without looking back though. I don't suppose there's anyone who can tell me that now."

CHAPTER THREE

Accustomed to getting up at five in the morning to work out or go for a run before going to the office with his great-grandfather, Jeremy was up before sunrise the following morning. Not wanting to disturb the family so early, he stayed in his room. Without knowing their routine, he didn't want to intrude.

It had been late when everyone finally went to bed. The house was silent this early. Had everyone slept in? On a ranch this size, there were probably ranch hands to take care of the everyday things. He had assumed this wasn't a family that relied on others to do the chores. But maybe he'd been wrong. He felt like a fish out of water trying to feel his way around. It wasn't easy fitting in with a group of strangers he just happened to be related to.

The window in his room faced the long drive leading up to the house. He could see cattle in the pasture across the road, but no one was attending them. Was that part of the Baker's ranch? There was a lot he didn't know about these people. The outbuildings were out of sight so he couldn't tell if there was any activity out there.

When he'd met Shep and Parker during the summer, he'd felt a connection with them. But had that been wishful thinking on his part? His family consisted of Jacob and Victoria. His parents were as much strangers to him as these people.

Yes, Victoria had several nieces and nephews, even some greats, one of which worked for Jacob. Kenneth had worked for the company since he graduated from college ten years ago. He knew as much about Fallon Industries as Jeremy did. Probably more, Jeremy admitted. He was the one who should take over when Jacob eventually retired.

Jacob barely recognized the time and effort Kenneth put into the company. He wasn't blood-related to the Fallons. That was all that mattered to the older man. With his heart set on Jeremy taking over, no one else mattered to him. Jeremy paced across the spacious room. He knew that wasn't what he wanted. Convincing the older man to let that idea go wasn't easy. He didn't want to hear it.

The house he'd grown up in was more of a hotel than a home. In the few short hours he'd spent at the ranch, he knew this was what he wanted, a place where even strangers felt comfortable and welcome. Had he come to Texas to find a place where he felt like he fit in?

Even while he'd been in college he felt this same restlessness. He hadn't known the cause or what to do about it though. Now maybe he had the answer. He wanted a place to belong, a place he could call home, a family, a real family.

He also knew he didn't want to spend eight to ten hours a day sitting behind a desk for the next fifty years. He wasn't cut out for that life. He wouldn't be a good CEO. He wanted to be *doing* something not just pushing papers around.

Years ago, Jacob had expanded the company, adding products that hadn't been available at the time it was founded. He wanted to do something similar, only on the production end, not in management. That isn't where his interests lie.

He had broached the subject several times while he was in college, but the conversation never went anywhere. Jacob simply wouldn't listen. Did he have the courage and the backbone to strike out on his own? He shook his head. That wasn't what was stopping him. Abandoning the company would break his great-grandparents' hearts. After all they'd done for him, would he be able to walk away like Barnard had done? The way his father had done?

He sighed. Break their hearts or spend the rest of his life trapped doing something that would make him miserable. What kind of choice was that?

When he heard the powerful engine of one of the large pickups he'd seen around the ranch roar to life, he put aside his personal dilemma. He needed coffee.

Stepping into the hallway at the same time as Bailey, his face lit up. "Good morning." The sun pouring in the window at the end of the hall struck her red hair, making it look like there was a red halo glowing around her head. A smile curved his lips at his fanciful thoughts.

"Well, good morning to you." She returned his smile. "Are you just getting up?"

"Um, no, I've been up..." Looking at his watch, he was surprised to see it was after eight-thirty. "I guess I've been up for several hours." He hadn't realized he'd been wrestling with his thoughts that long.

"Why didn't you come downstairs? You don't have to stand on ceremony around us. Everyone gets up early on a ranch." She cocked her head, looking up at him. A flirtatious grin curved her lips. "If I'd known you were up, I would have asked if you'd like to go for a ride with me."

He was surprised that she'd been up long enough to go for a ride. There was a lot he didn't know about living on a ranch or this family. He hadn't heard any activity in the house since he got up. Had he been so wrapped up in his thought that he'd missed the sound of doors opening and closing?

"Maybe we can do that tomorrow?" His words went up at the end, turning them into a question "Or some other time if you're going to be busy." He was still feeling his way around. He didn't want to presume her offer had been serious. Maybe she'd meant it as a polite way of brushing him off. Sort of like saying to someone, 'let's do lunch sometime'. Lunch never happened.

"I'm never too busy to go for a ride."

"I have to warn you, I've only been on a horse once. That was last summer with Shep."

She shrugged. "He's a good teacher." Flipping her red hair over her shoulder in a saucy manner, she batted her thick lashes at him. "I'm better." Laughing, she linked her arm through his as they started down the wide staircase.

Walking into the kitchen together, they interrupted a

passionate moment between Shep and Parker. "Oh, get a room," Bailey teased. "We have company."

"We have a room, remember?" He tugged at her long hair as she walked over to the coffee pot. "Besides, Jeremy isn't company, he's family."

The statement stunned Jeremy. It was that simple. He was family. They didn't have to put on airs or act differently around him. No matter what, you were still family. This was what a real family was like. A broad smile that looked remarkably like Shep's lifted the corners of Jeremy's lips.

This was what he was searching for. Family. He didn't doubt that Jacob and Victoria cared for him. But what would they do if he continued to reject the idea of running Fallon Industries? He didn't have the answer to that. Pushing the thought aside, he took the cup of coffee Bailey offered.

With his arm still around his wife, Shep turned to Jeremy. "Hope we didn't wake you."

"No, I've been up for a while," he admitted. "I didn't want to disturb anyone."

Shep chuckled. "You don't have to worry about that. We're all early risers here." He tugged at a lock of his sister's long hair. "Since when did you start sleeping late?"

"I'm not the one who's just comin' downstairs," Bailey scoffed. "I've already mucked out Windstar's stall and taken her out for a ride. What have you accomplished this morning?" Cocking her hip to one side, she rested her hand at her waist.

"I've had plenty to keep myself busy." He didn't need to explain. The blush on Parker's face did that for him. He turned to Jeremy. "You interested in another ridin' lesson later today?"

"I've already got that covered," Bailey said before Jeremy could say anything. "We have plenty of horses, but if you don't mind, I thought we'd take your mare," she said, looking at Parker. "She's really gentle."

Parker nodded her head, her red hair, so like Bailey's,

bounced around her face. "Not at all. I'm sure Lightening would enjoy it. I didn't have a lot of time to ride this past summer."

She looked at Jeremy to explain. "I was helping a friend get her old farmhouse ready for her granddaughter to move in." She chuckled. "It's a long story for another time. You're free to ride Lightning anytime. You don't have to ask me."

~~~

The next morning was Thanksgiving. Jeremy's stomach was jittery with nerves. There would be a lot of people at the ranch for their annual Thanksgiving bar-b-que. Before going down for breakfast, Jeremy called his great-grandparents to wish them a Happy Thanksgiving. They weren't thrilled that he was having a good time. He was sure they'd been hoping he'd be miserable.

"How can we be happy when you aren't here to celebrate with us?" Victoria had asked. She was good at piling on the guilt. Their celebrations had consisted of the three of them. Not much to be happy about.

"When are you coming home?" Jacob barked before he could say anything. "Your work is piling up." He wasn't so bad at the guilt trip either.

"How much work can there be?" he'd asked with a forced laugh. "I've only been gone a couple of days. I'm sure Kenneth can do his work and mine as well without breaking a sweat." That statement had been met with a long silence.

"Kenneth decided he needed to take some time off. The ingrate," Jacob finally muttered. "He could have waited for a better time since you decided to abandon us right now."

"I haven't abandoned you, and neither has Kenneth," he argued. "You can't actually believe he is ungrateful either. Other than you, he puts in more hours than anyone else in the company. That includes me," he added. "I can't remember the last time he took more than a few days off. He even comes in on weekends." He wanted to impress on the older couple how much Kenneth did for Fallon Industries.

"Well, he could have picked a better time," Jacob continued to grouse. "We need you to get back here."

Was something else going on? It wasn't like Kenneth to take time off, especially since he knew Jeremy would be gone. Maybe he was trying to impress upon Jacob exactly how much time and effort he put into the company. Jeremy didn't blame him in the least.

He dismissed those thoughts. Whatever was going on with Kenneth and his great-grandparents would have to wait. "You knew when I left that I would be gone for a month or better."

"You won't even be here for Christmas?" Victoria wailed. "What kind of Christmas will that be for us?"

Before he could answer, Jacob put in his two cents. "I suppose you've taken up with that bunch."

"If by taken up, you mean I like these people, you're right. I like them very much. That doesn't mean I like you and Great-grandmother any less." The thought of Bailey brought warmth to his face. He couldn't say how or why, but there was something about her that had drawn him in almost instantly.

Jacob harrumphed, but managed to refrain from saying anything more. Victoria wasn't finished laying on the guilt though. "We miss you, dear. You are the only family we have left. Your father is God only knows where. He doesn't even bother to call. At least you remembered us enough to call."

Jeremy sighed. This was getting out of hand. "Kenneth is also your family. You have other nieces and nephews as well. You could always invite some of them to visit." He knew that would never happen as long as Jacob had any say in the matter. The man thought the only people that mattered were Fallons.

Ending the call a few minutes later, Jeremy tried to shake off the depression it had left him with. If they were lonely and miserable, it is their fault, not mine, he told himself. They had cut everyone out of their lives but him. He would have to remind himself of that several times before he actually believed it.

The day had already started when he finally made his way to the kitchen. "Good morning, Jeremy." Mona smiled at him. "I hope you're ready for a Texas-style Thanksgiving. It gets pretty crazy around here."

"I'm looking forward to it. I'm willing to help with anything. I take instructions well."

After a hearty breakfast, he followed Shep outside where a group of men was putting up several large tents and canopies. "You do this every year?" There was a sense of wonder in his voice.

Shep nodded his head. "Yeah. Grams and Granddad started this when my dad was little. It seems to get bigger every year." He chuckled. "It was getting too much for them so the folks moved it here a few years back. It's not your typical Thanksgiving dinner with turkey and mashed potatoes. Everyone brings their favorite dish and we end up with plenty of leftovers. It can get a little overwhelming if you aren't used to crowds. Everyone manages to have a good time."

"In my family, four people is considered a crowd. Jacob and Victoria wouldn't know how to deal with any more than that."

"Your family is a lot bigger than you ever knew." Shep laughed. "I hope you'll stick around long enough to get used to us."

"Me, too." He knew this was what he'd been missing in his life. Family.

"What can I do to help?" If he was part of this family, he needed to pitch in. But he didn't want to get in the way. It was like watching a well-choreographed dance. Everyone knew their job without stepping on anyone's toes.

"We need to bring out the tables and chairs once the tents are up. The festivities start about four when a group of local musicians begins playing. We have a portable dance floor in the Quonset hut that needs to be put together. There are also propane heaters in case it turns off cold." He chuckled. "I know you think it's warm here even after dark, but Texans like it a little warmer than you're used to." He chuckled again.

Parker had helped out in the kitchen all morning. By mid-afternoon, she wanted to sit down with her feet up, but she didn't want anyone to think she was slacking. "I think we have this covered, dear." Mona stopped beside her. "You're lookin' a little overwhelmed. Why don't you go put your feet up for a little while?" After having five kids, she knew how her daughter-in-law was feeling.

It was as though Mona had read her mind. "Maybe I'll get my shower now. That should revive me." Placing a kiss on Mona's cheek, she headed up the stairs.

Coming back down a short time later, she was ready for the festivities to begin. People would start arriving soon. This was her second Thanksgiving at the ranch and it still amazed her. She missed her folks around the holidays, but they would be here in another couple of weeks. She had hoped Grandma and Grandpa would be here, but they were needed at home.

A smile curved her lips. Uncle Charlie and Betty's twins were so cute. At the thought of having her own baby, her hand automatically went to the baby bump filling out her shirt. In a few months, she'd have her own baby. She couldn't wait.

She'd called her parents that morning to wish them a Happy Thanksgiving. They were just as anxious to see her as she was to see them. Living so far away from her family was hard, but she couldn't give up the house Rosie had left for her and Shep. They'd make it work.

When people started arriving, she joined the others in the main tent. The temperature was still warm enough to leave the flaps on the tent up. As the temperature dropped, the men would lower two of the sides and light the propane heaters. The tent would be cozy or stifling, depending on your outlook.

Looking across the big tent at Jeremy, he seemed a little overwhelmed by the large crowd. "It takes a bit of getting used to," she whispered when she walked up to him. "I thought we had a lot of friends and family in Arizona, but this beats anything I've ever seen." Shaking her head, her red curls bounced around her face.

Jeremy nodded, understanding what she meant. "It must cost a fortune to do this every year. My great-grandfather would never do something like this for his employees." He sounded a little sad about that.

"How many people work for him?" No one had even thought to ask what kind of company he owned.

"There are more than two hundred employees right now."

"That's a fair-sized company." She looked up at him. "What kind of company is it?" She hoped he wouldn't think she was prying.

"At its inception, they started out making farm equipment. When Jacob took over close to sixty years ago, he expanded into mining equipment."

"Wow! That's impressive."

"I guess." He shrugged. He'd grown up around the company, working there during summer break from school. It didn't seem like a big deal to him. "I have a few ideas of my own that I would like to see implemented." He sighed. "So far, I haven't had any luck convincing Jacob to agree to that. As you can imagine, he doesn't take suggestions very well. He likes to think that he's the only one who knows what's best." He sighed again. "And not just for the company," he added softly.

"He expects you to take over from him, right?" Jeremy nodded his head. "How does he think you can run the company if he won't allow you to contribute anything?"

Jeremy shrugged. "To say he's a control freak is putting it mildly. At close to ninety, it's a little late to try changing his mind about anything."

Parker noted a trace of sadness in his voice. She wished there was something she could say to help. From the brief dealings they'd had with the man last summer, she knew Jacob would never change the way her grandpa had. She wondered what the story was that had made him so hard. She doubted that Jeremy knew the full story either. "How long has Fallon

Industries been in business?" she asked instead.

"Barnard's grandfather started it more than a hundred and fifty years ago. He wanted better products for the farmers in the area. Over the years, it's grown along with farming and mining methods. I like to think that our family has helped farmers all over the world to improve their crops. During both World Wars, the company switched to making anything to aid in the effort. I'm still not certain what all that entailed." He shook his head.

"How do you feel about taking over when your great-grandfather retires?" She tilted her head to the side, looking up at him. It was almost like talking to her husband, they were so much alike.

"If he has any say in it, he'll never retire, which suits me just fine." His voice dropped to a whisper on the last words. It wasn't exactly an answer, but it told the story.

"You don't sound like it's something you want."

"I've never really had an option about what I wanted to do with my life," he admitted. "It's always been a foregone conclusion that someday I'll be the head of Fallon Industries." He shrugged his broad shoulders to ease the tension that thought caused. "I don't mean to sound ungrateful. They've done everything for me. Until recently I wasn't sure what I wanted to do. Now…" He didn't finish the thought. He knew that sitting behind a desk for the next fifty years wasn't what he wanted out of life. The problem was telling his great-grandparents.

After a moment, he continued. "As Jacob reminds me regularly, I'm all that's left of the Fallon line. He expects me to carry on the tradition for future generations." His shoulders drooped slightly as though there was a heavy weight on them.

Looking up at him, an impish smile curved her lips. "Does that mean he expects you to get married and start producing heirs?" That sounded a little too close to what had happened in her mom's family.

He laughed. "I did ask him that recently. He told me not to

be brazen." His gaze turned to Bailey where she was helping her mother set out more food. He didn't have the best examples of marriage to learn from but suddenly the thought of getting married didn't seem so foreign. Maybe all it took was the right woman to change his mind.

Turning serious again, he shook his head. "I'm not sure what he expects other than for me to step into his shoes someday. I'm glad someday hasn't come yet." He released a heavy sigh. "Please don't think that I'm complaining because I'm not. It's just..." He didn't know how to describe how he felt part of the time.

"It's just that they've never let you do your own thing. It sounds like he expects you to live his life, not your own."

He thought about that for a moment, before nodding his head. "That pretty much sums it up." He shook off the depressing thoughts. "Enough of that. It looks like the party is in full swing." The musicians had set up in one of the tents and began playing a popular country song. The food tables were laden with every type of food imaginable. People were moving between the food tent and where the musicians were playing. He held out his arm to her. "Shall we join in?"

With a happy laugh, she took his proffered arm. "Yes, we shall. From the looks of those tables, there's enough food to feed a group twice this size."

"I've been wondering where you were." Bailey intercepted them on the way to the food. She smiled up at Jeremy. "What do you think of Thanksgiving Texas-style?" She linked her arm through his free arm.

"It's like something out of a movie," he answered with a chuckle. "I didn't know people had parties like this."

"This is nothing. Wait until you see the Fourth of July. The town holds a potluck in the courthouse square and nearly everybody in town joins in." She sounded like he was going to be here forever. "After dark, there are fireworks the likes you've never seen."

He looked at her expecting her to be joking. "But there are

five thousand people in Promise."

"And nearly twice that many when you count those of us living on ranches and such." She nodded her head.

"I drove by that square on my way through town. It isn't big enough to hold that many people."

Her lilting laugh was like a breath of fresh air. "Well, maybe I was exaggerating. Just a little," she added, holding up her thumb and forefinger, leaving a small space between them. "But it's a great time. You'll see."

"Maybe," he qualified his answer. He hadn't thought he'd be here any longer than a few weeks, through Christmas and New Year at the most. But this was where he wanted to be; where he was supposed to be. The realization staggered him for a moment, and Bailey looked up at him. "Are you okay?"

"Um, sure, I'm fine. Just tripped over my own feet." Now wasn't the time to consider where those thoughts came from or what they meant.

The two didn't even notice when Parker slipped her hand off his arm. A happy smile curved her lips. Maybe Bailey and Jeremy were meant for each other the way she and Shep were. Time would tell. She hoped he wouldn't run off right away. Jacob and Victoria hadn't allowed him the opportunity to explore anything other than what they wanted for him. This was his chance.

CHAPTER FOUR

Standing on the sidelines, Jeremy watched the activities. He'd spent the last hour dancing with all of Bailey's girlfriends when the only one he wanted to dance with was Bailey. It was the strangest thing. He'd only known her a little more than twenty-four hours yet it felt like he'd been searching for her his entire life. How could that be? He felt like the belle of the ball. He chuckled at himself. Was there even such the thing as a male belle of the ball?

"Howdy, there." A young man slapped him on the back startling him out of his reverie. "I'm Sam Weston," he held out his hand to Jeremy. "I'm Bailey's boyfriend." He clasped Jeremy's hand in a bone-crushing grip. He held on longer than was necessary. Jeremy wondered if they were in an arm-wrestling match.

"In your dreams, Sam, in your dreams." Bailey laughed as she strolled up beside them, linking her arm through Jeremy's. She had been watching all of her friends fawn over Jeremy, now Sam was making claims where he had no right.

For a long moment, Sam looked like he was going to explode. Just as quickly he chuckled. "You can't blame a guy for tryin'." He slapped Jeremy on the back again and swaggered off. It looked like he was playing John Wayne moving through a saloon in one of his many westerns.

"Um, I hope I didn't step on any toes." Jeremy thought Sam Weston's claim was a long-held wish for reality, not simply a dream.

"You didn't," she shrugged. "Just because we've been friends for years, he thinks that gives him some sort of privilege. He thinks more highly of himself than he should." With great effort, she forced herself to relax. "All of my girlfriends have monopolized your time tonight. I think it's my turn to dance with you."

"Why ma'am, it would be my pleasure," he said with an

exaggerated accent. With a sweeping bow, he led her onto the dance floor.

Sam watched as that city slicker swept a laughing Bailey into his arms. He should be the one dancin' with her, makin' her laugh, makin' her love him. All he'd wanted since junior high was for her to be in love with him. Instead, she falls all over that slick dude. I'll show him he can't get away with something like that.

There was a malevolent look in his light-colored eyes as he followed the couple on the dance floor. He needed to get out of there before he exploded. The guy didn't look like he could hold his own in a bar fight. A nasty chuckle erupted from his lips. He'd show the guy not to mess with another guy's girl.

Football was to Texas what hockey was to Canada. Sam loved playing and had enjoyed the attention it garnered him. But the one person he had been trying to impress hadn't taken notice. Watching her with that slick dude, he could picture slamming his fist into the guy's face.

"Hello, Sam." Giving a start when someone spoke to him, he turned to face Kylie Turner. "Sorry about that." She gave a small laugh. She didn't sound particularly sorry. Her gaze followed to where he'd been staring. "It doesn't look like your night has gone quite as you'd been hoping."

"Not quite," he agreed. "I saw you dancing with prince charming. That must have given you a thrill." His tone was snarky.

"It was expected of me." Kylie shrugged. "He was polite enough, but he wasn't interested in dancing with me." She looked up at him, a crooked grin on her lips. "He kept watching Bailey. How's that make you feel, being dumped for that guy?"

When he gave a low growl she giggled, enjoying his pain. "I'll bet you thought you'd be dancin' her right into your bed tonight." She watched his face to see his reaction.

"It's none of your business what I was thinkin', Kylie.

Was there somethin' you wanted?" Kylie was a pretty little thing, but she always had an agenda of some sort. He was never able to get a feel for what was on her mind.

Kylie shrugged, tilting her head to one side as she looked up at him. "I've never been able to figure out why you let her lead you around by your..." She paused slightly before finishing, "By your nose. I thought you were better than that. You should dump her snooty little ass."

"And take up with you?" he asked.

She shrugged. "You could do worse. So could I."

Sam wasn't paying attention. He was still watching Bailey. When the music ended, the couple walked off the dance floor. Jeremy's arm was around Bailey's waist. Sam's jaw clenched, the muscle in his cheek bunched up.

"These people think far too highly of themselves. It's time someone brought them down." She thought she was just the one to do it.

"Huh?" He turned his attention back to Kylie when he lost sight of Bailey in the crowd. "What did Bailey do to you?"

"She exists," Kylie stated simply. "I'm tired of playing second fiddle to the likes of her." Kylie's dad had moved them to Promise from Dallas two years ago. He had big plans of turning the ranch he bought into some fancy resort development for weekend cowboys. So far that was a bust.

"I wouldn't get any ideas of hurtin' her. She's the princess of this family. She's got four big brothers and they'd stomp you into the ground so fast it would make your head swim." He conveniently forgot his plans for making Bailey pay for dumping him for that city slicker. It was the worst thing he could think to call someone. Being from any city outside of Texas meant you weren't worth much.

"What?" Kylie arched a brow at him. "You gonna do something to stop me? I thought you'd want to get back at them for dissing you tonight."

"Yeah, I do, but it isn't her fault. He's managed to sway her thinkin'."

Kylie chuckled. The guy was delusional if he believed that. Bailey thought she was better than others because her family roots go deep in Texas soil. But folks had recently found out the truth. Her granddad was the bastard son of some woman in Iowa of all places. No one seemed to care one way or the other. Until recently, that is.

Turns out his birth mother was some famous author. That gave Bailey even more reason to think she was better than others in town. *And a small town at that*, Kylie thought with a sneer. She still lived on a ranch in the nowhere town of Promise, Texas.

She shuddered. She wanted to go back to Dallas where she belonged. That's where her friends were. She didn't want to be stuck out in the middle of nowhere for the rest of her life. In Dallas, Bailey wouldn't be so high and mighty. Her friends would put Bailey down in an instant.

"He's not gonna be here much longer," Sam muttered, breaking in on Kylie's thoughts. "He'll be gone before long. He isn't from Texas." That was a condemnation in itself. "Besides, he's some sort of relative."

"And you're thinkin' she's just gonna fall right into your arms when he's gone." She shook her head. This guy was dumber than a rock. Bailey was never going to go out with him. They'd been friends for a long time. If it was going to happen, it would have a long time ago. He would never be anything other than a friend to Princess Bailey, she sneered. Too bad he wasn't smart enough to see that simple fact.

Turning away, she shrugged. "See ya around. Sucker," she muttered softly. Just because he wanted to stick around and torture himself, didn't mean she had to watch. She was out of there.

~~~

The back of Jeremy's neck began to prickle, and he turned to find the cause. Sam Weston was leaning against the wall in a classic cowboy pose with one foot on the wall and his arms across his chest. All he was missing was the cigarette dangling from his lips and he could be the cowboy cutout sold in so many souvenir stores. There was a dark glare on his face. If looks could kill, Jeremy would already be dead.

Jeremy guessed that he'd played football and probably lifted weights. The lump on his nose spoke of a fight or two he'd been in. Jeremy gave a mental shrug. He might not have played football or been in any fights, but he did work out at the gym. He'd even taken boxing lessons in college. He wasn't looking to be in a fight with the guy, but he figured he could hold his own.

Turning away, he dismissed the man. He hadn't come to Texas to get in a fight or to fall in love. The first he'd pass on, but the second… If the feeling he got just being around Bailey was anything like love, he was all for it. A smile tilted the corners of his mouth.

"Fire! There's a fire in the field." The shout caught everyone's attention bringing the bar-b-que to a halt. Folks scrambled. Everyone knew the drill. This far out of town, waiting for the fire department to get there would be a disaster. The fire would be out of control by then.

Several guests were local firefighters. Within minutes they had a heavy-duty hose hooked up to a hydrant. The fire hadn't had time to spread and it wasn't long before the fire was out. Several of the men stayed in the field to make sure there weren't any hidden embers that could come to life later.

"How did that get started?" a man asked. Jeremy had been introduced to him earlier as Sheriff Jose Garcia. He'd been friendly at the time, but Jeremy saw a different side of him now. He was all sheriff. Jeremy wouldn't want to be a crook and come up against him.

"Did anyone see somebody in the field?" He looked around for any answers. There were so many people milling around, it would be difficult to know if someone had been in the field to cause mischief or were there for a few minutes of quiet.

All these people were friends of the Bakers. Would

someone deliberately set the fire? Maybe they'd been smoking and dropped their cigarette without making sure it was completely out. If that was the case, they wouldn't want to admit they were at fault.

Jeremy looked around for Sam. He didn't see him in the crowd, but that didn't mean he wasn't there. It didn't mean he'd set the fire either, Jeremy reminded himself. He hadn't been happy when Bailey denied his claim of being her boyfriend. But would he do something like that if he really cared for Bailey?

He looked around for Bailey. In the confusion, Jeremy had lost sight of her. His stomach clenched. Promise was a small town, but that didn't mean crimes like murder and kidnapping didn't happen. Small towns were no longer immune to crime. Was Sam upset enough at Bailey to want to harm her?

Before he could freak out, he saw her coming toward him from the barn. There was a relieved look on her face. "Sorry I deserted you," she said. "Horses are terrified of fire. I had to make sure they were all okay."

"The fire was on the opposite side from the barn. It couldn't reach them without going through a lot of people."

"I know," she shrugged. "They could still smell the smoke. I wanted to make sure they didn't begin to panic." She paused for a minute before going on. "In the past year or so, there has been a lot of vandalism. I wanted to make sure someone wasn't trying to distract everyone while they went after the horses."

"Why would someone want to hurt the horses?"

She lifted one shoulder. "As I said, we've had some vandalism recently."

"Just your ranch or other ranches as well?" He thought there was something she wasn't saying.

"Well, ours and Grams' and Granddads'. Some of the others that butt up to ours have been hit." She looked at the field where some of the men were still checking the fire area. "This is the first time something like this happened. It was mostly cut fences allowing the horses and cattle to get out. A couple of times we had sugar in the gas tanks."

"That sounds like a bunch of teenagers playing pranks." He frowned. "Why would they pick on your family?"

"I wish I knew." She sighed. Until recently, Promise had been relatively crime-free. She hoped this wasn't an indication of things to come.

Sam had been watching from the sidelines. As soon as the fire was noticed, Bailey took off for the barn while everyone else headed for the field. The horses were always her first concern. Sometimes he thought she cared more for the horses than she did for people. Or at least people who weren't part of her family.

He'd thought about going to help her, but figured she wouldn't welcome his intrusion. Besides, she had a way with the horses that he lacked. He was a rancher at heart, but horses weren't his only concern.

What about that dude? He didn't look like he knew his way around horses. If he couldn't ride, she'd dump him in a heartbeat. Maybe then she'd realize she should be paying attention to him, instead of some city slicker.

Once the fire was out, she was right back with that dude. A low growl escaped his lips. He wished he could dismiss her as easily as she dismissed him. He was becoming obsessed with having her.

But he wasn't the only one. It had been instant hate between Kylie and Bailey when Kylie's family moved to Promise a couple of years ago. Like a lot of the ranchers, Bailey didn't like the idea of turning a ranch into a resort development. Bailey had been as vocal about her opposition as her old man. He wasn't sure what Kylie thought of the idea, but that didn't seem to matter. She didn't like anything about Bailey.

Tonight wasn't the first time he'd heard Kylie say something against Bailey. She'd always made it clear she didn't like her. It had surprised him when she showed up.

Maybe she'd crashed the party? The thought intrigued him. How would Bailey feel about him if he exposed Kylie? It was worth thinking about.

It hadn't helped Sam's cause that his father was working with Kylie's on the resort development. His dad had struggled to make his ranch as successful as the Bakers. The land had been in his family for generations like the Bakers, but he didn't have the will to do what was needed to make a go of it. When Kylie's dad came around looking for somewhere to build his development, Sam's dad had jumped at the opportunity.

He had to make Bailey see he was on her side. He wanted to keep the land, but he didn't have a say in the matter. It was his father's ranch to do with as he pleased. If the land had belonged to him, would he have worked to keep it a ranch? Or would he have sold out like his dad? He didn't want to think about that. Besides, it was a done deal. In Bailey's eyes, his dad had sold out and was working with the enemy.

~~~

"Are you all right?" Shep wrapped his arms around Parker. "I can't believe something like this happened. Promise has never had a crime problem."

"Neither had Whitehaven," she said with a resigned sigh. "If Uncle Abner was here, he'd say it was my fault. He seems to think trouble follows me around like a shadow." Abner was her grandfather's brother, one of the grumpiest old men on the planet.

"He's beginning to come around," Shep joked. "I think you're beginning to win him over. It'll just take another fifty years."

Parker lifted one brow at him. Somewhere in his late seventies or early eighties, Abner was almost too old to change his ways. Shep shrugged, "It was worth a try."

Normally, Gus would be with her when there were strangers around. But these people were friends of his family. No one had a reason to harm Parker. Because of that, they thought Gus would be more of a problem than a deterrent to trouble and had decided to leave the dog in the house. Gus hadn't been happy with that decision. Now he wished Gus had been on patrol. No one would have gotten as close as the field without Gus giving a warning.

The fire hadn't been aimed at Parker, but she and their baby could have been hurt anyway. Until they figured out what or who had caused the fire, he'd make sure Gus never left Parker's side.

Maybe setting that fire had been a mistake, but it sure felt good. It would have been even better if it burned up the whole damn place. The sheriff questioned all the party-goers. They weren't going to be able to tell the sheriff anything. No one around here knows anything about my past. That means I can move around without anyone guessin' what I'm up to.

CHAPTER FIVE

"What's going on, Dad? You never said anything about having trouble until now." Shep was in the field where the fire started the night before with his dad, his younger brother Jordan, and Jeremy.

"I mentioned some vandalism goin' on." Dan sighed. "I thought it was just kids blowin' off steam durin' the summer." He looked around at the scorched winter grass. "This is somethin' different."

"Sugar in the gas tank wasn't the work of kids, Dad," Jordan said. "Besides, if any of the ranchers caught their kids doin' this stuff, those kids would be payin' for any repairs for the next year." He looked at his brother. "It took two days to round up the cattle and horses after the fences were cut."

"Whoever is behind all this has escalated to a new level," Dan agreed. "If someone hadn't spotted the fire when it first started, this could have been a whole lot worse.

"Is anyone else havin' trouble?" Shep frowned.

"Some," Dan admitted. "Mostly it's been our ranch and Grams and Granddad. I didn't know I'd made anyone mad enough to do somethin' like this though."

"You have any trouble with your vet clients? This seems personal." He pointed at the burned area. Jeremy agreed with Shep, but he kept his thoughts to himself. This was family business. They might say he is family, but he didn't think they would appreciate him stating his opinion.

Dan ran his long fingers through his hair. "As I said, I haven't had a run-in with anyone."

"What about Turner and Weston, Dad?" Jordan asked. "You've been against their development from the start."

"I've been friends with Elliott Weston for years. Other than bein' a little lazy, I had no problem with him until he sold off a big share of his ranch to put up those ugly mansions." He shook his head. "We're too far away from Dallas to think some of Weston's rich friends would want to move out here, even to play weekend cowboy."

"Weston?" Jeremy spoke up for the first time. "Is he related to a Sam Weston?"

"His son. Why?" Dan frowned at him.

"I met him at the bar-b-que last night."

"And?" Dan prompted. He didn't see what that had to do with the fire. Jeremy hesitated. Saying something against the son of one of Dan's friends might not be wise. "Spit out whatever you've got to say, son. At this point, I'm willin' to listen to anything."

Jeremy shrugged. "I'm not sure if the fire has anything to do with Sam." He nodded his head at the burned area.

"But it might?" Dan pressed, cocking his head to one side.

"I don't know. He told me he was Bailey's boyfriend, but…"

Dan barked out a laugh. "Not even close. Did Bailey hear him say that?" Jeremy nodded. "What did she have to say?"

"She set him straight on that matter. He isn't her boyfriend."

"How did he take it?"

For a minute Jeremy tried to come up with the right words for Sam's reaction. "At first he seemed upset, but then sort of laughed it off and just walked away."

"Did you see where he went after that?"

"Shortly before the fire started he was leaning against the wall of the house."

Dan frowned. "What was he doing?" He thought there was something else Jeremy wasn't saying.

Jeremy shrugged. "I got the impression he was watching Bailey and me. I'm not sure whether the daggers he was sending our way were for me, Bailey, or both of us. After the fire was discovered, I didn't see him again."

"Was he with anyone?"

Jeremy started to shake his head, then stopped. "There might have been a girl, young woman," he amended. "I think she was one of Bailey's girlfriends I'd danced with earlier in the evening. I didn't catch her name."

Dan scrubbed his hands over his face. He hadn't slept well after everyone left the night before and was up early to check out the burned area. He'd been hoping there would be some clue or something to say who had done this. But there was nothing. There wasn't even a cigarette to say it had been an accident. He was sure the fire had been deliberately set. What he couldn't figure out was why anyone would do it. Those people were his friends.

He didn't know if what Jeremy said about Sam had anything to do with the fire either. He'd disagreed with Sam's dad about selling land to Turner for his upscale development, but he didn't think Elliott Weston carried a grudge over it. He was simply too lazy. He still considered him and Sue Ann friends. They had been at the bar-b-que.

"There's nothing to be found out here," he finally said. "We might as well go back to the house and get some breakfast. There is as much work takin' everything down as there was settin' everythin' up." He sounded bone-weary. Was the bar-b-que worth all the work it took to put up and take down? *I'm just tired*, he told himself. *Once everything is back to normal and I've had a good night's sleep, I'll be able to put this into its proper perspective.*

~~~

Jeremy thought about what Dan had said. The vandalism started about a year ago. About the time all the information came out about Ralph Baker being the son of Barnard Fallon and Rosie Shepard. Was that a coincidence? He couldn't think of any reason someone would target the Bakers because of the relationship to the Fallons. Except his great-grandfather. The thought came out of nowhere.

What reason would Jacob have to set a fire in Dan's field? Of course, he wouldn't do something like that himself, but did he know people he could pay to do it for him? Jacob seldom did anything that didn't benefit him or Fallon Industries. The vandalism here wouldn't benefit Jacob in Kansas. It wouldn't change Jeremy's mind about taking over Fallon Industries.

Once everything was back to normal Shep went to search for his wife. He found her right where he expected: on the front porch swing.

At the farmhouse in Iowa, her favorite place to sit and read or just relax was the swing on the big porch. The warm Texas sun reminded her of the Arizona winters. She missed being in the desert, but he knew she wouldn't give up the house Rosie had left to them.

It was also one of his mom's favorite places to sit when she had a few minutes and he found the two women together. "If there isn't anything you need me to do right now, I'm gonna take Star Fire out. It's been a couple of days since he had a good run."

Mona looked at Parker before nodding her head. "We've all been so busy gettin' everythin' ready for the bar-b-que, I haven't had time to spend with Parker. This will give us a little quiet time together."

When Jeremy and Bailey pushed open the door, he grinned at Jeremy. "I was gonna see if you'd like to go with me, but I see someone else beat me to it." He winked at his sister.

Shep placed a kiss on his wife's lips. "I love you," he whispered. Before he could step down from the porch, Gus whined.

"I think there's someone else willing to go with you." Parker laughed.

"Sorry, buddy, you need to stay here and guard Parker." The big dog's ears drooped as though he'd just taken a beating.

"That's nonsense," Parker said. "The fire had nothing to do with me. Gus needs the exercise as much as Star Fire."

Shep debated what to do before finally giving in. He leaned down to scratch the big dog's head. "All right, boy, let's go see if Star Fire is ready to stretch his legs." After placing another kiss on Parker's lips, he headed down the steps with Gus happily at his heels. Jeremy and Bailey were close behind.

Parker watched the young couple, a happy smile lifting the corners of her mouth. "They make a cute couple," she said, turning to her mother-in-law.

"Yes, they do," Mona agreed. A worried frown drew her brows together.

"You don't like that idea?" Parker asked.

Mona tried to shrug off the worry that was tugging at her. "Bailey has never been serious about any of the boys she's dated. I can see she thinks a lot of Jeremy, but he's only here for a short time. If she really cares for him, her heart will be broken when he leaves. On the other hand, his heart will be broken if he falls harder for her than she does for him. I don't want either of them getting hurt. That isn't up to me," she said with a sigh. "I have to believe God will lead both of them in the right direction."

Parker silently agreed. She was sure there was someone else that would try very hard to stop any sort of relationship from building between Jeremy and Bailey. Mr. Fallon had big plans for Jeremy. It didn't matter what Jeremy wanted. She didn't know why people tried to control the people they were supposed to love.

If Rosie's father hadn't tried to force her into a loveless marriage, there was no telling how things would have turned out for them. But if she and Barnard had gotten married, there would be no Baker family and no Shep. Where would that have left her? She was grateful that God was in charge. He could turn the evil done by men into good.

Shep took his time getting Star Fire saddled letting Bailey and Jeremy get their horses ready first. He didn't want Bailey thinking he was following them. It was easy to see what Jeremy was feeling toward his sister was how he'd felt about Parker when they first met. He prayed they would have the same happy ending.

But would Jacob Fallon allow that to happen? Was Jeremy

strong enough to stand up to his great-grandfather? He shook his head. He'd have to leave all that in God's hands. It wasn't up to him.

Standing outside the big barn doors, Shep looked out over the field. He missed being here with his family, being on the ranch. But he also loved his work in Iowa. The house Rosie had left to Parker and him was home now. He'd put his sweat into turning it into the showplace Rosie had planned for it to become. With a baby on the way, their life was about to take a new direction. He couldn't wait.

Gus whined and Star Fire snorted getting his attention. They were tired of waiting for him. "Okay, guys. I get the message. Let's go." He swung up into the saddle. Star Fire took off at an easy lope before he was even settled on the horse's broad back.

Giving the big stallion his head, they raced across the open pasture. Gus had no trouble keeping up. When Star Fire finally slowed to an easy gallop, Shep decided to check the fence line as long as they were out. Private land and fences didn't stop teenagers with ATV's and dirt bikes from trespassing. They either cut the fences or knocked them down. Even some hunters didn't abide by the no hunting signs posted on the ranch. Was the fire the result of trespassers, or was it something more sinister?

A sharp bark from Gus drew his attention away from the fences. The big dog was prancing around, getting in the way of where Star Fire was trying to go. "What's the matter, boy?" He took a closer look at his surroundings. Just the other day, a mountain lion had attacked several animals on another ranch. If that was the case now, Star Fire would sense the danger. The only thing upsetting him was Gus getting in his way.

"What's wrong, Gus? Do you see something out there?" Was the person that set the fire the night before out for more mischief? Where were Bailey and Jeremy? He didn't want them to become targets.

He shifted in the saddle to see what was bothering Gus.

The sharp retort from a rifle and the searing pain of a bullet striking him in the shoulder were simultaneous. Shep slumped forward in the saddle, hanging onto the saddle horn to keep from falling off. The reins dropped from his grasp, trailing on the ground.

Star Fire reared nearly unseating Shep a second time. Gus was in a frenzy torn between going after the person shooting at them, and staying close to Shep. His training won out. He was meant to protect those he cared about. Picking up the reins Shep had dropped in his mouth, Gus led the horse toward the ranch house. Instinctively, he knew not to go so fast that Shep would fall off.

Mona and Parker were still sitting on the porch when they heard the sharp retort from the rifle. "What was that?" Parker sat up straight, while Mona stood up.

"It was a gunshot," Mona said. "Bailey and Shep wouldn't go riding without their rifles. Maybe one of them was shooting at the cougar." At least that's what she hoped it was. After the fire the night before, she had her doubts. Someone had deliberately set the fire.

Jordan had heard the gunshot as well and quickly saddled up his horse. Bailey and Jeremy had also heard the gunshot, and rode up like the devil was on their heels. "What happened?" Bailey shouted. "Was someone hurt?" After the fire the night before everyone was on pins and needles.

Coming close enough to the barn to be heard, Gus dropped the reins and began barking again. He still wouldn't leave Shep's side. His frantic barks focused their attention on the figure slumped over Star Fire's neck. "Mom, call 911," Jordan shouted over his shoulder. He could see the blood running down Shep's arm. Gus had picked up the reins again and began leading the horse toward Jordan.

Bailey and Jeremy reached Shep at the same time Jordan did. Jeremy helped get Shep out of the saddle. Mona called 911 as she and Parker ran to the big SUV. It would take too long for an ambulance to get to the ranch from town. Shep needed attention now.

As Jeremy and Jordan were loading him into the back of the big SUV, Dan's pickup pulled into the lane. One look at his son told him this wasn't the time for questions. "Let's go," he barked at the others. He climbed in the back with Shep. He might not be a medical doctor, but at least he could stop the bleeding.

Jose Garcia was waiting at the hospital when they pulled in twenty minutes later. "What happened?"

"Don't know." Dan shook his head. Worry was etched on his face. Emergency personnel whisked Shep away leaving the family standing in the waiting room. He wanted to follow but knew he needed to stay where he was. He hadn't been home when it happened. He let the others explain.

"Someone shot Shep while he was out ridin'," Mona explained. "He'd been gone thirty, forty minutes when we heard a gunshot. Before anyone could go out to see if Shep had spotted a mountain lion, Gus led Star Fire in. Shep was slumped over his neck." Remembering the blood running down her son's arm, her voice broke. That was all anyone knew right then. They would have to wait until Shep regained consciousness.

CHAPTER SIX

"Where the hell were you last night?" Roger Turner growled at his daughter when she came down for breakfast. It was already ten in the morning, and she was just getting up. He hoped she kept better hours at college than she did at home. He wasn't going to foot the bill for her to party for the next four years.

"Out," Kylie answered flippantly. "I wanted to see… some people." Calling anyone in this godforsaken place a friend went too far. She wouldn't even call them acquaintances. "There was something I needed to do."

"Like what?"

"Stuff. I'm nineteen. I don't have to give you an accounting of my time." It had been his idea to move here, not hers. She didn't know why she even came here for the holiday. This certainly wasn't home.

"As long as I'm footin' the bills, you'll tell me where you're goin' and who you're goin' with. If you don't like that idea, you can get a job. Then you won't have to tell me anythin'." He glared at her. When he got angry, the Texas drawl he'd worked hard to eradicate from his voice returned.

Kylie had always been rebellious, but it had gotten worse after her mother died and they moved to Promise. It had seemed like a good idea at the time. Now he wasn't so sure.

He'd been threatening to cut off her allowance for the last two years. She didn't think he'd do it, but she didn't want to put him to the test either. "Yes, Dad. I'm sorry."

If she was trying to sound contrite, she missed the mark by a mile, but Roger was willing to accept it at face value. "So, where were you last night? I thought we'd have a nice Thanksgiving dinner just the two of us."

"I thought Miranda was here." She ignored his question about where she was. Miranda Fulsome was their latest housekeeper and his current mistress.

"Why would you think Miranda would be here? I suppose she was with her family." He always thought she wasn't aware of his sleeping habits. He was learning how wrong he was about that as well as so many other things where his daughter was concerned.

"I saw her car leaving as I pulled up to the house," she stated, glancing over her shoulder at her dad. There was a snide grin on her face.

A red blush crept over his cheeks. Clearing his throat, he asked again, "Where were you last night?" His question circled back around. She had avoided answering long enough.

After pouring herself a cup of coffee, she turned around to face him, leaning against the counter. "I went to the Baker's bar-b-que."

"Why the hell would you do that?" he snapped. "Were you invited?"

"Heavens no," she laughed. "They wouldn't invite the likes of us." She included him in her statement. "I just thought you might be interested in knowin' that your business partner and his family were there."

That gave him a few heart palpitations. Of course, he knew that Weston was on friendly terms with Baker. But considering the way Baker felt about Weston selling him some of his land, he didn't think Weston would be on the guest list. "Nothin' wrong with that," he said as casually as possible. "They've known each other for years." He tried to put a good face on things.

She shrugged. "I guess you didn't hear what happened then." Dropping that teaser, she turned to take her coffee into the other room.

"What happened? Was someone hurt?" That wouldn't be a good thing. If Baker thought he was behind it, he'd come after him. He had enough trouble without adding to them.

"Someone tried to set their field on fire."

Roger's eyes grew large in his face. "Was anyone hurt? Did they see who did it?"

She lifted one shoulder in a slight shrug. "I was getting ready to leave when it happened. I don't think anyone was hurt. I'm not sure if they saw… who did it." She knew how to imply something making it sound true.

His eyes narrowed. "Did you set the fire?" He wasn't sure what her hints were leading up to.

"Why, Daddy, how could you ask such a thing?"

Her pretend innocence didn't fool him for a minute. He thought she was capable of just about anything if she thought it would get her what she wanted. He just didn't know what she would get out of doing something like that.

"I wouldn't have brought it up if I'd known you were gonna accuse me of bein' an arsonist." Crocodile tears illuminated in her violet eyes. Setting down the half-full coffee mug, she fled the room.

"Honey, I'm sorry. I didn't mean it like that." Roger pushed himself out of the chair. He considered going after her but stopped himself. This was just another way she had to get what she wanted. He wasn't going to fall for it this time.

She slammed the door to her room. He was going to pay for that. Of course, she hadn't set the damn fire. But even if she had, he had no right to accuse her.

He cringed when the door banged shut. That hadn't gone so well. What was he supposed to do with her? She had a mind of her own. He'd been hoping she would stick around today. He had some investors coming to look at some property. Their son would be with them and he wanted Kylie to be there. *She could sell sand to an Arab,* he thought. But not if she was mad at him.

Wentworth's son liked horses. He was looking for property to indulge the kid. That's where Kylie came in. Not that she liked horses. He laughed at the idea. She hated everything to do with living in Promise and that included horses. But she was a good actress and could pretend for an hour or so. He even kept a horse in the stable to impress investors and buyers.

He sighed. A horse was an added expense he could barely afford at the moment, but having a horse in the pasture looked good to prospective buyers. After all, didn't weekend cowboys want a place to show off their horses? He'd made sure the small ranches he planned to set up had room for at least one horse.

People were moving from both coasts due to high taxes and other things they didn't like. They were moving to Texas in droves. He wanted to cash in on the mini-land rush. Anyone could make money on real estate. So far, this ranch had been a money pit though.

Getting this house built had taken longer than he'd expected due to several 'accidents'. Baker wasn't the only one that didn't want him to succeed. He'd managed to keep those problems quiet, but he was running out of money. It had taken all of his wife's life insurance money to buy that stupid ranch from Weston. Too bad he hadn't had the foresight to take out more before it was too late. He needed to sell more of those stupid mini-ranches.

Maybe folks from New York and California weren't interested in horses. God knew his own daughter wasn't and she was a born and bred Texan like him. The fact that he wasn't interested in horses either, slipped past him.

~~~

"What can you tell me, Shep?" It had taken a lot longer than Jose wanted before he could question the younger man. He wasn't sure if Shep would even be able to tell him anything.

Their county was far enough from the border to miss the worst of the drug smugglers and human traffickers, but Promise wasn't as crime-free as it used to be. Still, he couldn't see how the vandalism and now the fire and this had anything to do with illegals crossing the border.

He'd been the sheriff for the past ten years. Before that he'd been a deputy. He'd been friends with the Baker family most of his life. Something like this shouldn't happen.

Shep started to shrug but stopped wincing at the pain the movement caused. The shot had been a through-and-through and hadn't required surgery, but he'd lost a lot of blood. *And it hurt like hell*, he added silently. "I can't tell you much, Jose. I was checking fences when Gus started to act up. At first, I thought maybe there was a cougar close by. But Star Fire wasn't concerned. Just as I turned around to see what had Gus so upset, I heard the shot. I nearly got knocked off the horse when the bullet hit me."

Lost in the memory, he'd forgotten Parker was sitting in the chair beside the bed until she gasped. "Sorry, Darlin'." He took her hand. Turning back to the sheriff, he shook his head. "That's all I know. I didn't see anyone or hear anything until Gus started actin' up. That's when I was shot. I don't remember anythin' after that until I got here."

"Too bad I can't interrogate the dog," the sheriff groused. "I'll bet he'd have plenty to say." He gave a heavy sigh. With nothing more to learn from Shep, he went to talk to the others in the waiting room.

He looked at the worried faces of the group gathered there. Eyeing the newest member of the Baker clan, he wondered if Shep had been shot by mistake. When he'd met the man at the bar-b-que, the resemblance to Shep had been shocking. In the light of day, he could notice the differences. But at a distance, someone could easily mistake Shep for Jeremy.

"Mind if I ask a few questions?" He pulled up a chair to face the group. Dan and Mona were itching to get to see their son. He wasn't sure how they would take him questioning the young man, but it was necessary. "Can you think of a reason someone would take a shot at Shep? He hasn't lived in Texas for a long time." He didn't look directly at Jeremy but watched for his reaction out of the corner of his eyes.

They all shook their heads. "Would anyone from Iowa have a big enough grudge against him to follow him to Texas?" Again there were head shakes all around.

Now for the tough one, he thought as he turned to Jeremy.

"What about you? You got any enemies willing to take a shot at you?"

"What?" Jeremy drew back in the chair. "I've never even been to Texas until a few days ago. The only people I know here are the Bakers. Unless you count all the people I met at the bar-b-que. But I don't think I made any enemies then." Remembering the incident with Sam Weston caused him to sit up straighter. Would Sam shoot him because he was with Bailey? Even for the old west that seemed a little extreme.

"What are you thinkin', son? Something came to mind."

"I really don't think it's worth mentioning." Jeremy shook his head. Speaking against the son of one of Dan's friends wasn't a good way to stay on their good side.

"Let me be the judge of that," Jose said. There was little doubt that he wasn't taking no for an answer.

Jeremy glanced at Bailey. What would she think of what he had to say next? Giving a mental shrug, he answered the sheriff. "Someone at the bar-b-que wasn't happy that I was there."

"Sam?" Bailey frowned. "He wouldn't shoot you because of me. We've never even gone out on a date." That wasn't because Sam hadn't asked. She always turned him down.

Jose shifted his attention to her. "Humor me. Tell me what happened?"

Jeremy let her do the talking. She could put the right spin on what happened. "There isn't much to tell, Sheriff." When he was in cop mode, she addressed him appropriately. "Sam told Jeremy he is my boyfriend. I set him straight." She lifted one shoulder in a shrug. "He walked away and I didn't see him again."

"What about you?" He looked at Jeremy. "Did you see him after that?"

"Across the yard, but I didn't talk to him again." He'd already told Dan about the incident earlier that morning. He didn't think it amounted to much.

Dan and Mona hadn't said anything through this. Now

Dan stood up. "We took Gus out to the field this morning. He wasn't able to lead us anywhere. There wasn't anything to tell us who set the fire. We'll take him out to where this happened, but first I need to see my son."

Jose nodded his head. "Let me know when you're ready to go. I want to have a look around as well." It was clear that he wasn't going to let Dan go alone. He was a fair man, but when it came to his kids, he didn't allow anyone to mess with them. If Sam Weston was behind the fire and now shooting Shep, that young man was in for a heap of trouble.

Turning back to Jeremy, he said, "So you don't have any enemies?" He didn't exactly believe that. Everyone has enemies.

"I haven't been in Texas long enough to make enemies," he stated indignantly.

"What about back home? Anyone there who'd like to get even with you for something in the past."

"No, I..." He stopped. What about the man who stopped him on the street when he left the diner?

"Somethin' come to mind?" The sheriff cocked his head to one side again.

"Yeah, but not back home. I don't know who the guy is. He was in the diner where I stopped when I drove into town. When I left he was waiting for me."

"What'd he want?"

"I'm not real sure what he wanted. After he heard the waitress say my name, he kept staring at me." He shook his head. "He wasn't just staring, he was glaring at me. When I left, he stopped me and told me my dad is a prick." He gave a dry chuckle. "I had to agree with him." He shrugged. "He didn't bother to give me his name."

"You think he might take a shot at you because of your dad?" the sheriff asked. That was a little farfetched, but people did strange things all the time.

Jeremy shrugged. "I have no idea. He said my dad ruined his life. I don't know when this was supposed to have happened. I don't think my dad has ever been in Texas, and he hasn't been in Kansas for more than five years."

"I'll talk to Erma Jean. She might know who it was. Did he follow you out of the diner?"

Jeremy shook his head. "No, he left before I did. He was waiting for me when I walked out."

Jose stood up. "Thanks for takin' the time to talk to me. I'll see what I can find out." He looked at Jordan and Bailey. "Tell your dad I'll be out at the ranch when he's ready. Maybe that dog can lead us somewhere." He put the big cowboy hat on his head and left.

~~~

"I'm goin' to be okay, Darlin'," Shep assured Parker once they were alone. "The bullet didn't hit any vital organs." The bullet had passed through his shoulder without doing a lot of damage. He'd lost some blood, but the doctor assured everyone that he was going to make a full recovery. "It's hunting season," he said. "It was probably a hunter." It was an easy explanation, but he wasn't convinced. Neither was the sheriff. He wasn't sure Parker bought that story either. His shoulder would be immobilized for a while, but it wouldn't keep him down permanently.

She glared at him. "I don't care who it was. People can't go around shooting at the first thing that moves. What was a hunter doing on the ranch anyway?" Her green eyes flashed with anger even as they filled with tears. "I can't lose you," she whispered.

"You aren't gonna lose me. If Gus hadn't started actin' up..." He swallowed hard thinking about where that bullet might have gone if Gus hadn't kept Star Fire dancing around. "If it weren't for Gus and Star Fire, I'd be in a lot worse shape."

"They have to catch whoever did this."

"We will," Dan assured her as he and Mona pushed aside the curtain separating the small examination rooms. His tone was hard and his face was dark with suppressed anger while

Mona's was white with worry.

She crossed to the opposite side of the bed, taking Shep's hand. "I thought I wouldn't have to worry about someone shooting at you after you got out of the Army." Tears formed in her eyes.

"Hey, where's that pioneer spirit everyone in Texas always talks about," Shep teased.

"Shep, this isn't funny," she scolded as tears ran down her face. He might be a grown man, but he was still one of her babies. When she found out who did this, he might have a few new holes in his hide as well.

"I'm sure it was an accident, Mom. It's hunting season." He tried to deflect her worry as well as Parker's.

"Don't give me that load of crap. Everyone knows we don't allow hunters to come on our land. There are signs posted everywhere warning trespassers will be prosecuted."

Closing his eyes, he sighed. His argument wasn't convincing anyone. "When are they letting me out of here?" He changed the subject. "I'm ready to go home. Lyin' on the ground would be softer than this bed."

"Sorry, Shep, you're going to our guest for the night. I want to keep an eye on you." The doctor had entered the small cubical without him noticing.

"That's not gonna happen," Shep stated, rolling his head on the hard pillow. "I'll sleep a lot better in my own bed."

"Your bed is in Iowa," Mona reminded him. "You need to listen to the doctor."

He shook his head again sending a stray lock of dark hair over his forehead. A stubborn set to his jaw told them he wasn't going to give in. Dr. Carson sighed. He'd dealt with a lot of stubborn patience over the years, and this man rated right up at the top. "If I release you, you have to promise you aren't going to do anything more strenuous than lift a fork." He gave Shep a stern look.

"I promise I won't let him out of bed," Parker assured the doctor. That brought snickers all around, and her red cheeks matched her red hair. "You know what I meant." She kept her eyes trained on her hand clasped in Shep's.

The doctor coughed to disguise his chuckle. "Yes, we know what you meant." He looked at Dan to keep from laughing at her embarrassment. "I'll leave it to y'all to make sure he stays down. If he tears those stitches loose, he'll be right back here."

Turning back to Shep, he continued. "I want to see you again in three days. If there's any sign of infection, I want you back here before that." He gave Shep a stern look. "If that happens, I won't be so lenient then. I'll keep you here for a week."

"Got it, doc. I promise to be a good boy." He held up his good hand as though making a vow.

The nurse turned out to be a harder nut to crack. She wasn't going to let him walk out of the hospital under his own steam. "It's the wheelchair, or you stay here." She crossed her arms over her ample chest. "Your choice."

After several long moments of a staring contest, Parker leaned down to whisper in his ear. "Give it up, Honey. She's got you over a barrel. It's the wheelchair and home or you stay here. I've always heard that nurses run a hospital, not the doctors. I don't think she agrees with the doc's decision."

With a loud harrumph, he stood up and quickly sat down in the wheelchair. His head swam dizzyingly, but he tried not to let on.

"Not as smart as you thought you were." The nurse chuckled. His face was pasty white. "Aren't you glad I insisted on the wheelchair?" She didn't wait for him to answer as she gave the chair a push.

~~~

Watching as a caravan of trucks pulled out of the hospital parking lot a few minutes later anger bubbled up inside. The entire Baker clan had been at the hospital.

Just like most of my life, that hadn't gone as I'd planned. What am I going to do now? They'll be looking for the shooter. I can't get caught, not yet. Everyone has to pay for the way he treated me. This just means I'll have to wait a little longer. But nothing is going to get in my way. People needed to pay.

CHAPTER SEVEN

Sam waited until he saw Roger Turner's fancy car pull out of the lane before heading up to the house. After ringing the door chimes, he waited for Kylie to come downstairs. The house was big enough for two families to live there without running into each other. Why did they need something this big for just two people?

He rang the bell again with the same results. Her car was sitting out front. She didn't ride the lone horse her dad kept for show, and she didn't walk anywhere. Waiting for what felt like hours, he knew she was home. Pressing his finger on the bell, he could hear the constant chime deep within the house.

After another five minutes, he got worried. Had something happened to her? What would her dad do if what Sam suspected was true? He pounded on the heavy door. "Come on, Kylie, I know you're in there. Open up." He tried the door handle just in case. Most folks on the ranches didn't bother locking their doors. But the Turners weren't ranchers. They were city folks. Of course, the door was locked.

Pressing on the bell button again, he raised his fist to pound on the door just as it swung open. "What the hell do you think you're doing?" Kylie stood on the threshold, her hands braced on her hips.

"What took you so long to answer the door?" He pushed his way past her into the impressive foyer. This wasn't the first time he'd been in the house, but the grandeur of the foyer alone was enough to steal his breath.

"Did it ever occur to you that I didn't want to see anyone? What are you doing here?"

Looking around, his mouth hung open. "Huh?" He snapped his mouth shut. "What'd you say?"

"I asked what you're doing here."

"Did you set that fire last night?"

"What fire? I don't know what you're talking about."

"Right after you left, someone set Baker's field on fire. Did you do that?" Her pretend innocence didn't fool him. She had to know about the fire.

"Why would I do something like that?" She frowned at him as much for his accusation as for the way he was snooping around.

It must have cost a million dollars to build this place, he thought. Turner must be made of money to have a place like this after buying part of the Weston ranch. Sam wasn't sure how much Turner had paid his old man, but it was a bundle. Maybe this was why his dad had sold off more than half their ranch to this crook. He wanted something bigger, better.

The original Weston house had been built seventy years ago by his great-grandfather when he first came to Texas. Sam's dad tore down the house he'd grown up in to put up something better when he took over the ranch from his dad. He had big plans but very little carry through. Elliott Weston wasn't cut out to be a rancher. He could never make it work.

Sam sighed. He sure wouldn't mind livin' in a place like this. If all the houses Turner built were like this, the resort development might not be so bad after all. "Is this what your house in Dallas was like?" He looked over his shoulder at Kylie.

"Did you come here to accuse me of arson or to gawk at the house? You've been here before."

"This is a mansion or a palace," he whispered.

"Yeah, and I'm a princess," she said sarcastically. "Now get out. You can't come here and accuse me of something and then stare at my house like it's some sort of showplace."

"It is a showplace," Sam said. "All you have to do is look around Promise. There isn't another place like this anywhere. Even those houses your dad is building don't look like this. And I wasn't accusing you of setting the fire. I was just askin'. That's all."

"Fine, you asked and I answered. Now get out." She held the door open for him, tapping her foot impatiently."

When the door slammed shut, he realized she hadn't answered him about the fire. She was pretty good at sidestepping an issue. He was going to have to keep an eye on her. Why would she set a fire at the Baker's ranch?

So who did set that fire? Why would anyone want to hurt the Bakers? *Besides me, that is,* he thought. But it wasn't the Bakers he wanted to hurt. It was that damn Fallon guy. If he hadn't shown up, Sam might have a chance with Bailey. Or was he deluding himself?

Noticing a vehicle behind his truck, he checked his rearview mirror. The sheriff's car was right behind him. Out of habit he checked how fast he was going, and groaned. He was going ten miles over the limit. Easing off on the gas, he hoped the sheriff hadn't been clocking him. If he got another speeding ticket, his dad said he'd take away his truck. "I'm not a kid," he muttered. "He can't tell me what to do." But that never stopped the old man from tryin'.

"Damn." The sheriff pulled into the lane leading up to his house right behind him. There would be no escaping. Elliott Weston was sitting on the front porch. Why wasn't he working instead of lounging around? That was the problem. His dad didn't want to work on the ranch. If he did... Sam gave up thinking about the ifs in his life.

"Howdy, Jose," Elliott greeted the sheriff from the porch. He didn't bother getting up. He'd been enjoying the warm sun while having a beer. "What has my son done this time?" Sam held his breath waiting for the ax to fall.

"Nothin', Elliott. I just have a couple of questions for him." The sheriff turned to Sam. "Wondered if you could tell me where you were about ten this mornin'."

Afraid the sheriff was gonna give him a ticket right in front of his dad, Sam's breath came out on a whoosh. This wasn't about his habit of speeding after all. "Right here. Why? What's this about?"

"You were just comin' home from somewhere. Where were you?"

Beads of sweat broke out on Sam's forehead. Had Kylie called the sheriff after he left there? She would think it funny if she could get him in trouble. "Um, I just went for a drive. What's this about?" he asked again.

"What were you doing before that?" Jose looked at Elliott. "Was he workin' with you on the range?" If Sam hadn't taken the shot at Shep thinking it was Jeremy, he might have seen someone else.

Elliott barked out a laugh. "Don't recall the last time either of us was on the range. He isn't much for workin' with the cattle."

"What cattle?" Sam asked, his tone a touch snarky. "You sold off the last of the cattle when you sold half the ranch to Turner." His voice was bitter. It was useless arguing the point though. There was nothing he could do about it now. His dad was clueless where his family was concerned. He saw Turner's resort development as a way to get rich quick. This was just the latest in a long string of ideas that never panned out. It probably wouldn't work out any different from the rest.

"So he was workin' with you around here about that time?" Jose pressed.

Elliott scratched his head. "Can't rightly say what the boy was up to. Today is a holiday, so I haven't done much work myself." It sounded like Elliott was willing to throw his son under the bus if it kept suspicion away from himself.

Sam snorted. His dad was supposed to be a partner with Roger Turner in this resort development. He didn't see either of them doing any actual work. At least Turner was out trying to sell people on his resort idea. Elliott's only contribution was selling the guy a big chunk of land.

There were only three horses left in the stable. He didn't remember the last time his dad took one of them out. Since he had let the two remaining ranch hands go after selling out, any work required around the place fell on Sam and his mom. Elliott was waiting for 'his ship to come in' as he put it. Sam thought that ship would likely sink because his dad wasn't willing to put in the effort to make it happen.

Sam's mom pushed open the door, stepping out onto the porch. "Mornin' Sheriff. What brings you 'round on a holiday?" The woman was short and stocky, the opposite of her husband's long, lanky form. They were sort of like Jack Spratt and his wife from the nursery rhymes. He thought she was also the driving force behind the family.

"Just followin' up on a few things. Have any of you thought more about that fire at the Baker's last night? Do you remember seein' anyone out in that field before the fire started?" He watched for any sign that they knew more than they were telling.

Sam looked at his parents. They both shook their head. He wasn't sure where they'd been when the fire started. He hadn't seen anyone in the field, but he hadn't been looking either. He'd been watching Bailey with that dude.

He still suspected Kylie might have started it since it started shortly after she said she was going home. That was why he went to see her that morning. She didn't exactly deny setting the fire, but that didn't mean it was true. She only had a passing acquaintance with the truth. He kept his doubts to himself. Crossing Kylie never came to anything good. She had a vindictive streak in her. He didn't understand why she had bothered to crash the party. She didn't even like Bailey.

The two were like oil and water. They had clashed from Kylie's first day at school two years ago. Kylie wasn't the easiest person to make friends with. He couldn't think of anyone in or around Promise she liked. She wanted to go back to Dallas. Starting a fire in the Baker's field wouldn't accomplish that. He shook his head. What was it the sheriff really wanted to know?

"What's the fire last night got to do with you askin' what Sam was doin' this mornin'?" Lost in his thoughts, Sam gave a start when Sue Ann spoke up. A frown creased her forehead. Jose knew she was protective of Sam to the point of being overbearing at times.

Jose shrugged his broad shoulders. "Shep Baker was shot this mornin' about that time."

Sam sat down on the step with a thud, but Sue Ann took several steps toward the sheriff. "And you think Sam had sumthin to do with that?" Her hands were braced on her broad hips. "He's a good boy. Why would he want to shoot Shep?" She was like a mama bear protecting her cub.

"Calm down, Sue Ann," Elliott drawled. "Sheriff's just doin' his job. Right, Jose?" A frown wrinkled his normally smooth forehead.

Jose shrugged. "Sure enough. Just askin' questions, that's all. Not sure if the shootin' has anythin' to do with the fire last night. Thought I should check it out with folks that were there."

"Maybe you should talk to those that weren't there," Sue Ann suggested. Her tone was mild, but there was still a fierce look in her eyes. "Maybe someone took offense at not bein' invited to the big to do. Some folks don't like havin' it rubbed in their face that others look down on them. After Elliott here sold off his land to that Turner guy, I was surprised we got an invite. Dan Baker made it clear he didn't want this resort to happen."

Whoa, where did that come from? Sam stared at her with his mouth hanging open. His mom was normally the most even-tempered person he knew. That little tirade was totally out of character.

Jose didn't know if Sue Ann was mad at the Bakers for opposing her husband, or her husband for selling the land. But she was mad at someone. Still, he couldn't see her shooting someone no matter how upset she was at them. He thought she'd probably take a pot shot at Elliott first.

Sue Ann's face grew pink with embarrassment. "I'm sorry," she stated sheepishly. She was unable to look the sheriff in the eye. "I saw some folks earlier in the week and they were complainin' about not bein' invited to the big shindig at the Lazy B. I guess I got caught up in that. The

Bakers have always been our friends, 'specially with Bailey and Sam bein' an item." A smile lit up her plain face when she looked at her son.

Sam's face turned every shade of red. He couldn't believe she had just said that. Okay, so he'd told her he was going out with Bailey when he was really going out with some buddies. He knew she would be upset if she knew the truth. She wasn't happy with some of the guys he palled around with.

Jose looked at Sam, one eyebrow raised slightly. That wasn't the story he got from Bailey. From the look on Sam's face, he thought Bailey's version was more accurate than Sue Ann's.

"Who was complaining about not bein' invited?" He turned his attention back to Sue Ann. "It might be worth talkin' to a few of those folks."

"Oh, really, Sheriff, please don't. They were just spoutin' off. It didn't amount to much. I'm sure they wouldn't do nothin' like shootin' at Shep. He doesn't even live in Promise now. They got no reason to shoot him."

Jose lifted one shoulder. "Probably not, but I gotta cover all the bases, as they say." When he let the silence draw out, she began to squirm. The best way to get someone to talk was to remain silent. They would say anything to fill that uncomfortable silence.

At last, she gave him a couple of names, but he couldn't see any of them complainin' about not bein' invited to the bar-b-que. He let that slide for now.

Turning back to Sam, he circled back to his original question. "So what were you doing about ten this morning?" It was after eleven when he saw him leaving the Turner place. It would be nice to know what time he got there.

"He was helpin' me with some chores around here until a short time ago," Sue Ann spoke up before Sam said anything. "I keep him pretty busy most days."

Sam whirled around to stare at her causing Jose to doubt Sue Ann's words. She was fiercely protective of her son.

Instead of arguing the point at the moment, he decided to accept her words. "Well, thanks for the information. Sorry if I disturbed your weekend." He looked at Sam. "It's right nice of you to help your ma out. Ranchin' is a rough life."

When Sam's face turned pink Jose was convinced Sue Ann had lied. He'd wait until he had the young man alone to question him further. "A young man needs to get out with his friends every now and again," he went on like he believed every word. "Is that where you were comin' from when I saw you on the road?"

Sam shook his head. "Um, ah, no, after I um, finished helpin' ma, I just took a ride. In my truck," he hastily added. "I was comin' home when you started followin' me."

Jose nodded his head. "Speakin' of that, you need to watch your speed. I'll let you off this time," he added when Elliott's face got red. That wasn't why he was there. "Mind tellin' me who you were visitin'?" He'd bet money the boy had been coming from the Turner place when he spotted him. That was shortly before eleven-thirty. It would be interesting to know what time he got to the Turner house.

"Um," Sam stammered, casting a glance at his mom. "Just a friend." Jose waited, hoping the silence would prompt him to say something. "Um, I stopped by the Turner's place," he finally said.

Both of his parents took notice of that. "What were doin' there?" Elliott sat up straight in his chair. "You don't need to bother Turner about this project."

A smile tugged at Jose's lips. He'd bet money Sam hadn't gone to see that particular Turner. From the look on Sue Ann's face, she had come to the same conclusion. And she wasn't happy about it either.

He'd been surprised when he saw Kylie and Sam together at the Lazy B the night before. It would be interestin' to know if she had been invited or if she crashed it. He didn't think Bailey would invite her. The girl had a knack for makin' trouble.

Taking several steps away from the porch, he turned back around acting like something else just occurred to him. "Is Bill Hancock around? I'd like to have a word with him." He looked toward the barn.

Elliott shrugged. "Haven't seen him since I let him go a couple of months back. Only got three horses left. Sam and his ma can take care of them. Don't need a ranch hand when I sold off the cattle." He barked out a laugh.

"You know where he's workin' now?"

"Don't know, don't care," Elliott said. "I'm not payin' his wages now."

Elliott had always been lazy, but since Turner paid him a bucket full of money for half of his ranch, he was even lazier. Jose shook his head. He sort of felt sorry for Hancock. The guy was a loner, drifting from one job to the next. But he thought he'd worked for Weston for several years. Touching the wide brim of his Stetson, he sauntered back to his SUV.

CHAPTER EIGHT

"You need to lie down, Sweetheart." Parker urged Shep toward the stairs.

"Will you lie down with me?" He waggled his eyebrows at her suggestively. "You look tired. I think you should take a nap." He wrapped his good arm around her shoulder. Each step was a little harder for him to take, but he tried to hide that fact from her. By the time they reached the top step, he was leaning heavily on her. The hallway ahead of him looked a mile long.

"Will you finally admit that you should have stayed in the hospital?" she whispered once the door was closed behind them. "You don't have to put on a show of how macho you are. I already know that." He started to speak, and she put her fingers over his lips. "I'm not going to fall apart. I'm a lot stronger than you give me credit for being. Yes, I'm a little more emotional now than I usually am, but I'm not going to break."

Kissing her fingers that lingered over his lips, he eased himself down onto the bed with a sigh. "Okay, you've made your point. I still didn't want to stay in the hospital. I hate hospitals." An involuntary shudder shook his body. He patted the bed beside him. "Lay down with me. I promise I won't get frisky." He sighed again. "I think I'm all out of frisky today." He closed his eyes. Within minutes his even breathing told her he was asleep.

Placing a soft kiss on his cheek, she tiptoed out of the room. She was emotionally spent, but she didn't want to disturb him. She would rest later. Right now, she needed to call her folks to let them know what happened. It would be good to have her mom here right now, but she needed to be strong for Shep.

"Hi, Honey, how are you? I was just getting ready to call you." Laura sounded excited.

"Um, I'm okay, Mom. I wanted to let you know about what happened." She paused, trying to frame the shooting so it didn't upset her mom.

"What's wrong? Is someone sick? Are you all right? Did something happen to the baby?"

So much for not wanting to worry her mom, Parker thought. "Shep was out for a ride this morning. A hunter must have thought he was a deer or something." Laura gasped. "He's okay," she hastened to add. "The bullet went through his shoulder without hitting anything vital. He won't be riding for a while. Or lifting a hammer," she added. She was trying to put a good spin on what happened, but she couldn't stop the tears from leaking down her face.

"What was a hunter doing on the ranch?" Laura asked. "Does Dan allow people to hunt that close to the house?"

"No, he doesn't. He and Jordan are out now trying to find any clues. They took Gus, hoping he could lead them to where the shooter… um, hunter was." She was using the excuse Shep had given even though she didn't buy it.

"What about the police? Shouldn't they be out there trying to find out who did this?" Laura asked indignantly.

Once she was assured that Shep was going to be okay and law enforcement was on top of what happened, Laura remembered why she had been about to call. "The boys finished their classes early," she said, her excitement tempered by what happened to Shep. It had been months since she'd seen her daughter. She couldn't wait to see her, especially in light of what had happened to Shep.

"That means we can leave early. We were able to change our airline reservations without any problems. We'll leave as soon as…" She stopped herself from finishing her thought. "This can't be a good time for Mona and Dan to have company. Maybe we shouldn't come now?" It was a question. She wanted to see her daughter, but she would understand that more company would be an added burden on Mona and Dan.

"Oh." Parker hadn't considered that possibility. "Um, I'm

sure it will be fine."

"No, honey. Before you say that, you need to check with Mona. We can wait until after Christmas and fly directly to Iowa and see you there." Her voice was thick with tears. She wanted to be with Parker at a time like this.

No matter how old you are, you still need your mom in times of trouble or excitement. This was a little of both. She wanted her mom here, but she couldn't impose on her in-laws either. While she was talking to her mom, Parker walked into the kitchen where Mona was standing at the sink. A worried frown etched lines on her normally smooth face.

"Um." She hesitated when Mona turned to look at her. "Mom wanted to know if they should cancel their trip here. She would understand after what happened today."

"Nonsense." Mona gave her a weak yet sincere smile. "Family should be together in good times and bad. I imagine you're wishing she was here right now. I know how much you're looking forward to seeing your folks. Shep is going to be fine. He'll be up and around by the time they get here."

"Well, that's the thing; the twins finished their classes early. They can change their reservations." She didn't say they already had changed them. "They would be able to come on Monday." She held her breath. She didn't want Mona to change her mind, but she would understand if she did.

"Monday will be fine. By then Shep will be driving everyone crazy from all the attention he's getting. I hope they'll reconsider staying here at the ranch with us. We have plenty of room." She spoke loud enough for Laura to hear her through the phone.

The ranch house wasn't as big as the house Parker and Shep had inherited from Rosie, but there were six bedrooms and a large den that could quickly be turned into another bedroom. There was also the bunkhouse for any overflow guests. The twins had wanted to stay there the last time the Evans family visited.

"We'll see when we get there," Laura hedged. "I don't

want to impose on you." The conversation was now between the two women. In the three years since Parker and Shep got married, the two families had become close. Laura was also looking forward to meeting Jeremy.

"You won't be imposing," Mona assured her. "We'd love to have you stay here. That will save you driving back and forth from town all the time." They visited for a few more minutes before Mona turned the phone over to Parker again.

Excited about her family's earlier arrival, she headed upstairs to check on Shep. If he was still asleep, she'd let him be. Silently opening the door to their bedroom, she peeked around the door.

Shep was lying on his back, his good arm tucked under his head staring at the ceiling. "Hi there, Darlin', did you come to join me after all?" Some color had returned to his cheeks along with the teasing note in his voice.

"Why aren't you still asleep? I didn't expect you to get up for another hour at least."

"I got lonely." He patted the side of the bed. "How are you feelin'?"

"I'm not the one that got shot," she chided him. Trying to sit up, he grimaced at the sharp pain in his shoulder. "Hold on there. The doctor said you were supposed to stay quiet for a few days."

"He said quiet, not bedridden. If you make me stay here all by myself, I'll never recover." He put on such a sad face she couldn't help but laugh at him.

"All right, I'll help you downstairs, but then you have to sit. You can't be up doing anything." She started to help him sit up, but instead he pulled her onto the bed with him. His lips captured hers in a passion-filled kiss. After a moment of surprise at the quick move, she settled into the embrace.

The thought of how close she'd come to losing him was like a physical pain in her chest. This must have been how Rosie had felt when she lost Barnard. For several long moments, she clung to him as though she'd never let go.

When she finally allowed him to pull away, they were both breathing heavily. "I don't think I'm up to much more than that right now," he admitted sheepishly. "Give me a couple of days?" His crooked grin tugged at her heart.

"I'll give you the rest of my life. I'm so glad you're going to be okay." Once again her emotions got the best of her, and she battled back the tears that burned the back of her eyes.

"Hey there, no tears. I'm fine. A little thing like this isn't gonna keep me down."

"A little thing?" she asked indignantly. "Someone shot you. And don't give me that nonsense about a hunter. You know as well as I do it wasn't a hunter. Your dad and brother are out looking for the culprit right now. I think I even saw Sheriff Garcia's SUV pull in a little while ago."

"I hope they took Gus. He'll be able to lead them to where it happened and where the guy was when he shot me. I wouldn't mind havin' a few words with him myself." His eyes grew dark thinking about what he would say to the guy.

She lifted one eyebrow. "What happened to your story that it was a hunter? You kept insisting it was just an accident."

"Oh, well, um, ah, sure." His face got hot. "I didn't want to worry you. You were right. I don't think it was a hunter. I don't think anyone would mistake me for a deer," he admitted sheepishly. "Even though the ranch is well posted that hunting is not allowed, we still get one or two every year that think no one will notice if they come on our land."

Now that he admitted it wasn't a hunter, she had some questions. "Who would shoot you? You haven't lived here for a long time. No one would carry a grudge that long."

"I have no idea." A frustrated sigh escaped his full lips. "I have no idea who would want to shoot me." He didn't want to talk about this any longer. "How about helping your husband get up before I get the idea I can finish what I tried to start a few minutes ago." He waggled his eyebrows at her making her laugh.

Before she helped him sit up, she looked at him, a serious

expression on her face. "Does this have anything to do with the fire last night?"

"That's another question I can't answer. I don't know anyone with a grudge against me or my folks." They hadn't heard what Jeremy said about Sam Weston or the man in town the day he arrived.

"I was so afraid I'd lost you." Her green eyes were bright with unshed tears.

Gathering her close with his good arm, he rested his lips against her forehead. "I don't know if these things are connected. I've known the sheriff for a long time. He's good at his job. He'll figure it out." He didn't know what was going on, but it needed to stop before someone else got seriously hurt.

"What are you doing out of bed? The doctor said you were supposed to rest." Mona's hands were braced on her hips when she saw Parker helping Shep down the stairs.

"I got lonesome up there all by myself, and I couldn't convince my wife to keep me company."

"Don't give me that sad face," she admonished him. "I'm onto all of your tricks to get your own way. You aren't so big that I can't wallop you if you misbehave."

"You wouldn't do that to an injured man, now would you?" He placed a kiss on her soft cheek.

"Oh, go on with you." She swatted his backside. "I'll bring some iced tea out to the porch." Heading back to the kitchen, she shook her head. He was as incorrigible as ever. He had always been able to twist her around his finger with that mischievous smile of his. She wouldn't have him any other way.

In between kisses, Parker told him about her family's early arrival. "Will it be too much for you if they come early?"

Shep laughed. "You keep tellin' me you aren't made of glass so stop fussin'. Well, I'm not made of glass either. I'm glad they can get here early. It will give everyone somethin' different to think about. Now stop fussin'." He placed a light kiss on her lips.

Shep struggled to stand up when the small posse of five rode up to the barn. He wanted to know if they'd found anything. Gus came up on the porch, plopping down at Parker's feet.

The sheriff stopped at the base of the steps while Dan and Jordan led the horses back to the barn. "Wonder if I could have a few words with Jeremy. Is he around?"

Jeremy hadn't joined Dan and the others when they went out to where Shep had been shot. His riding skills weren't up to theirs and he would hold them back. Hearing his name, Jeremy stepped out onto the porch. "Good morning, Sheriff."

The sheriff touched the brim of his hat before stepping down off his horse. "I talked to Erma Jean at the diner. She said the man starin' at you was Bill Hancock. Does that name mean anythin' to you?"

Jeremy shook his head. "Sorry, Sheriff. I don't recall the name. Who is he?"

"An all-around ranch hand," he answered. "He worked for the Westons until a few months ago."

"Did he tell you what he has against my father?"

"That's the thing, he hasn't been in town since that day he talked to you."

Jeremy shook his head. "I don't know how my father would know a ranch hand. To the best of my knowledge, he's never been on a horse or a ranch."

"You think your dad would remember him?"

Jeremy gave a humorless laugh. "I have no idea. I haven't seen him in five years. He rarely contacts me or my great-grandparents. I don't even know where he is right now. He pictures himself something of an art expert. The last I heard, he puts buyers and sellers together for a commission. He moves around a lot."

That wasn't what Jose wanted to hear. If he knew what Hancock had against the younger man's dad, he might be able to figure out who shot Shep and why. Before Shep had a chance to question him about what they found, he headed back to his SUV.

"I need to talk to Dad. I'll be right back." Shep had taken two steps when he swayed slightly.

"You aren't going anywhere. I'll bring him to you. Now sit down." The words were just short of an order. Gus let out a sharp bark as though reinforcing Parker's words.

"Yes, Ma'am." He gave a mock salute but sat back in the swing with a sigh. As much as he wanted to pretend being shot didn't affect him, he also couldn't deny he was weak. That fact angered him as much as being shot. Parker was right. He hadn't lived in Texas for a long time. He didn't have any enemies that he knew of, here or in Iowa. So why had someone shot him?

Entering the barn where Dan and Jordan were brushing down their horses, Parker's stomach rebelled. The fresh hay the men had spread around the stalls earlier couldn't mask the smell of manure in the wheel barrel standing at the back door of the barn. Maybe she should have waited for them to come up to the house.

"Are you okay?" Dan looked up from where he was working. "You're lookin' a little green." A frown creased his forehead.

"It's um, ah...." She swallowed the bile trying to force its way out of her throat. "I just need some fresh air." She headed out of the barn before she tossed her cookies. How embarrassing would that be? Drawing in several big gulps of air, she wrapped her arms around her stomach to settle it down.

"Parker, what's wrong? Dad, help her." Shep shouted. Watching from the porch, he cursed the fact that he couldn't get to Parker. The distance from the porch to the barn might as well have been across the country. He simply couldn't do that on his own at the moment.

Dan swept her up in his arms, to carry her over to the porch. "Please, you don't need to fuss. I'm fine," she protested. It felt like her face was on fire with embarrassment. "It's no big deal. I just wasn't expecting the smell to get to me."

Dan ignored her protests, setting her gently onto the swing beside Shep. Hearing Shep's shout, Mona rushed out to the porch. "What happened? Are you all right?" She knelt down in front of her daughter-in-law.

"Please, I feel like an idiot. It was just the smell of the horses."

Mona laughed. "Honey, it wasn't the horses that bothered you. It was what they leave behind. Can't say as I blame you either. Horse manure isn't an attractive smell especially for you right now. No more barn duty for you this trip." She leaned closer to Parker. "Consider yourself lucky. For the first four months with all of ours, I couldn't even cook breakfast, and sometimes even dinner and supper." She shuddered at the memory. She looked at her son. His face was as white as Parkers. "She's goin' to be all right." She patted his knee. "Come on, I'll fix you both some hot tea. It will help settle you both." They still had iced tea in their glasses, but hot tea would settle Parker's stomach.

CHAPTER NINE

"What happened out there? You nearly scared the life out of me." Shep gave his wife a sharp look.

"Now you know how I felt when Gus led Star Fire into the yard with you slumped over the saddle." Tears sparkled in her green eyes.

"Don't change the subject," Shep admonished. "I thought you were either going to pass out or have a miscarriage, and there wasn't anything I could do." His face was white at the memory of seeing her with her arms wrapped around her midsection. The thought of losing her or the baby was enough to bring him to his knees.

"Apparently, food isn't what's going to give me problems," she admitted with a chuckle. "The smell of horse manure on the other hand doesn't sit too well." She gave him a weak smile.

He sighed, cradling her against his side with his good arm. "No more barn for you." He echoed his mom's words. With her safe by his side, he closed his eyes.

Mona carried out a tray with glasses and a pitcher of iced tea along with a mug of hot tea for Parker. "I take it you didn't find anything worthwhile out there." She looked at her husband.

Dan shook his head, raking his fingers through his hair. "Gus led us to the spot where Shep…" Mona cleared her throat, dipping her head slightly in Parker's direction. Her face had gone pale again. "Where Gus distracted Star Fire," Dan finished.

"Nothing much there to see." The muscles in his jaw bunched up remembering the sight of his son's blood on the ground. "I don't know how, but Gus was able to lead us to where the guy was waiting."

"How did he know where I would be?" Shep asked. "I didn't have any destination in mind when I left the barn."

"That's something we'll have to ask him when we catch him," Dan said with a resigned sigh. "He'd stayed out of sight in the trees until you came into range." He looked at his son. "The leaves and pine needles were trampled down. It looked like he'd been there for a while. With a good scope, he might have been able to watch as you left the barn and track you as you rode out. It looks like he's a good hunter. All he had to do was wait until you got in range. There wasn't any shell casing, so he policed his brass."

"Are you thinking he's former military or police of some type?" Going back to the time he'd spent in the Army, there were several people he hadn't gotten along with, even a sergeant or two. But that was a long time ago. He dismissed those from his thoughts.

Dan shrugged. "I wish I had an answer. He turned to Jeremy. "Do you think your great-grandparents would be able to tell you how to get in touch with your dad? He might be able to give us some insight into why Hancock would want to hurt you." If the shooter was Hancock, he silently qualified. He didn't know why the man would want to hurt Jeremy or Shep.

"I'm sorry. Jacob and Victoria don't know anything more about where he is than I do. I haven't seen him in several years. He doesn't come back to the states very often. He doesn't want to end up trapped into working for Great-grandfather any more than I do." Until the last words had slipped out he hadn't realized that was exactly what he was feeling: trapped. He needed to fix the situation with Jacob before their relationship became as fractured as his dad's relationship with everyone else.

~~~

Mona waited until she and Dan were alone to ask more questions. "The blood trail would have led us to where Shep was shot even without Gus," he answered before she could voice her question. "Shep lost a lot of blood." His hands curled into fists. "It's a damned good thing Shep was able to stay in the saddle. He was a long way from the house. There's no telling whether Star Fire would have come back to the barn or stayed with Shep. By that time it might have been too late." His voice shook at the thought of a much different outcome. It was enough to bring a man to his knees.

He pushed that thought aside. "Whoever it was drove right through a fence. There were tire tracks where he'd parked his truck. No tellin' how long he sat up there waitin' for Shep to go for a ride. I'd sure like to have five minutes with the son of a ..."

Mona took his hand. "Jose is a good sheriff. He'll catch whoever did this. You can't go all vigilante. I don't want you sittin' behind bars for beatin' the guy to a bloody pulp. That won't solve anything."

Dan stood up, kissing the top of his wife's head. "I know, but it sure would feel good to get in one solid punch." He drew in a calming breath. "Jose took impressions of the tire tracks. I'm not sure if he will be able to trace the tire tracks to a specific vehicle."

Shep wasn't one to stay down for long. He insisted on going to the barn to check on Star Fire first thing the next morning despite his wife's and mother's objections. "I'm fine. I promise I won't do anything the doctor wouldn't like."

"Yeah right," Mona mumbled. "These Baker men are too stubborn for their own good." Frustration was making everyone short-tempered.

"And you wouldn't have it any other way," Lena chuckled. She and Ralph had come over first thing to help with the invalid. The only help Mona needed was trying to keep Shep down. Ralph was still getting to know Jeremy. "Shep might be stubborn, but he's also smart. He isn't going to do anything that will do more damage to his shoulder. He has a company that he loves to run and a wife and a baby on the way."

Mona sighed, smiling at her mother-in-law. "You're right. I know you are, but it's so frustrating when I also know he shouldn't be doing anything right now. I'll be glad when

Parker's family gets here. They should give him something different to think about."

Lena wasn't sure more people would help keep her grandson down or give him more reasons to be up and about. But Mona was right. With the family history they were learning about, it was no wonder the Baker boys, all of them, were stubborn. Rosie had to be stubborn to survive.

When Jeremy's phone vibrated in his pocket, he reached for it out of habit instead of necessity. Looking at caller ID, he wished he'd ignored it. Walking around the side of the house, he accepted the call. Ignoring Jacob was never a good idea, even on the phone.

"A fire, and now someone gets shot," Jacob started in before Jeremy even said hello. "It's like the wild west down there. You need to come home."

Jeremy frowned. "How do you know about all that?" There was no reason for either incident to make the news in Kansas. "Are you spying on me?"

"Not spying, protecting," Jacob stated. "You need to come home.

"Call it what you want, it still amounts to the same thing. Call off whoever it is. Now."

"Calm down. It's for your own protection."

"Call them off or I'm never going back there."

"Is that an ultimatum?" Jacob snapped. The boy was getting too independent.

"No, it's a fact. Either you stop this immediately, or you'll never see me again. Maybe this is why Barnard took off years ago and now my father. No one wants to have every aspect of their life controlled. Do it, or else." He didn't give Jacob a chance to respond before disconnecting the call. He felt like throwing the phone away.

The phone vibrated in his hand immediately. Jeremy debated whether to answer it or not. Waiting until just before the call went to voice mail, he accepted the call. He didn't say anything, letting Jacob wonder if he was there or not.

"All right, you win." It was probably the first time the older man had ever conceded in an argument.

"I win what?" Jeremy wasn't cutting him any slack.

"I'll call the investigator and tell him the assignment is over. You have to know that I was only doing it for your own good. Can't you see that those people aren't our type?"

"What exactly is "our type"?" He waited for Jacob to answer. When he didn't say anything, Jeremy continued. "What else has your investigator told you?"

Jacob chuckled. "I thought you didn't want to know. Maybe it's a good thing I had someone down there."

"It's never a good thing when you spy on people. You might find out something you don't want to know."

"What have you done that I wouldn't want to know?" He was suddenly suspicious.

Jeremy was tempted to tell him about Bailey, but as yet there wasn't anything to tell. He'd only been at the ranch four days. That certainly wasn't long enough to fall in love with someone. But it was long enough to know it was a possibility in the future. Instead, he said, "I've probably done a lot of things that you wouldn't approve of. Unless you had someone spying on me while I was at the university?" It was a question.

"I had no reason to have someone protecting you then. You were working hard to learn what is needed to run this company."

Jeremy sighed. "That isn't why I went to the university. I went there to learn what I could do in this life. One thing I'm not going to do is take over Fallon Industry. I don't want the job, and I wouldn't be good at it. Now, call that person off before I change my mind about a lot of other things. Tell Great-grandmother hello for me." Once again, he disconnected the call before Jacob could reply.

He waited to see if Jacob would call again. When the phone remained silent, he gave a satisfied nod. Hopefully, Jacob would finally listen to reason. But he wasn't one to listen to anyone else's reasoning.

It wasn't like he'd done anything in college that would upset Jacob. He'd still been the good little robot, following orders his great-grandfather gave. The unsettled feeling hadn't started all at once. It crept up on him a little at a time.

The culmination of all his feelings came to a head as he learned more about Barnard. If his father was anything like Jacob, Jeremy couldn't blame him for leaving the way he had. It was too bad though that he'd lost his life just when he found his freedom. He could only hope the same didn't happen to him now that he was on the verge of his own freedom.

CHAPTER TEN

Gus started barking in the middle of the night, pacing between the bed and the door. The only time he made a ruckus at night was when there was trouble. Shep groaned when he tried to sit up. "Stay where you are," Parker urged her husband not to get up. "I'll go see what's wrong."

"Don't go outside. Get my dad." His voice was sharper than he intended. He hated the fact that he had to rely on someone else to protect her right now.

Wrapping her robe around her, she opened the bedroom door. Gus tore down the stairs ready to take on whoever was causing trouble outside. Dan was already in the hall along with everyone else in the house. "Call the sheriff's office," Dan told Mona. "Stay up here." There was no doubt it was an order. Giving Jordan a nod to follow him, they headed down the stairs. They both were carrying guns. Gus was a trained guard dog; he'd corner anyone out there.

Gus was barking his own orders at the door. He wanted out. Someone was messing around with his people and he was going to protect them. By the time the men made it downstairs, they heard the roar of a powerful engine come to life. All they saw was a cloud of dust trailing behind a large truck.

Ten minutes later the sheriff's big SUV pulled into the lane. "What happened?" Jose stepped out of his vehicle. Someone broke into Jeremy's rental car. There was broken glass on the ground to attest to that. There was more glass on the back seat.

Jose turned to Jeremy. "Was anything important in the car?"

Jeremy thought about that for a moment then shook his head. "I think the only thing I left in there was a windbreaker from the university. It had my name stitched on the front."

"Well, if someone wears it around town, we'll know who

broke into your car." There were a lot of strange things happening since this young man arrived. He was going to keep an eye on him. Whether this was his doing or someone wanted retribution for something his dad did was up in the air.

"I have to report this to the rental company," Jeremy said.

Jose nodded "Just wait until after the lab gets here to take fingerprints. I'm not sure how much good that will do. Most vandals are smart enough to wear gloves. Maybe we'll get lucky and this was a dumb vandal."

The shooting had gotten everyone's attention. That wasn't the purpose, but it was interesting to see their reaction. Wait until they learn the rest of the story. Landing in Promise, Texas, with all these people had to be a stroke of fate. How else could anyone explain it? Maybe the right person hadn't been shot, but that was okay. They were all the same. They all came from Fallon stock.

The past was just that, the past. But keeping it there wasn't easy. Life here had been good. If the story about Rosie Shepard and Barnard Fallon had never come out, life could have continued as it was. But now that the cat was out of the bag there was no putting it back in. People needed to pay.

A case of nerves settled over Jeremy. Jacob and Victoria weren't much for religion. Jacob preferred to rely on himself than what he called a mythical being in the sky. Victoria had occasionally taken him to church when he was little. But that was a long time ago. Jeremy knew there was more to life than right here on earth. He just didn't know what to call it.

The last time he'd been in a church was for the funeral of one of his classmates in college. After partying all night at a frat house, he'd missed a curve, wrapping his car around a light pole at sixty miles per hour. But this wasn't a funeral. He wasn't sure what to expect.

A lot of the people attending the service had been guests at the bar-b-que. There had been so many people, he couldn't remember names, but most of the faces were familiar.

The back of his neck pricked and he looked around to see if someone was watching him. Had Jacob called off the person he'd paid to follow him? Jacob didn't like taking orders from anyone, especially not Jeremy. *He needs to understand that I'm serious,* he told himself. *I'm not taking over Fallon Industries.*

Spotting Sam Weston and his mom across the courtyard he figured that Sam was the cause for the feeling of being watched. He couldn't miss the glare the other man was sending his way.

Mrs. Weston rushed over to ask how Shep was doing. She was a sturdy woman. The term 'built like a fire plug' came to Jeremy's mind. She barely came to her son's shoulder. Sam had her solid build, so maybe he got his height from his dad.

Sam didn't bother joining his mom. Bailey had no right embarrassing him the way she did in front of that city slicker. He'd had a crush on her since eighth grade. Why couldn't she see that? He'd played football in high school, but wasn't a star. Still, he had his share of girls falling all over him. Just not the one he wanted.

He'd been upset when his dad sold off half of the ranch that had been in their family for generations. His mom had been even more upset. She was the rancher, not his dad. She had been the driving force behind what got done on the ranch. His dad was too lazy to make things work. Maybe Bailey saw that and didn't want to get mixed up with someone like that. His hands curled into fists.

If the resort development his dad was working on took off, they might be millionaires. At least, that's what his dad was hoping for. But his dad needed to put a little more effort into it. So far, Roger Turner had done all the work, and it still wasn't going anywhere. He sighed. He was doomed to be at the bottom of the ladder no matter what he did.

Jeremy was glad Sam Weston and his mom had gone in a different direction when they went inside. He didn't want to sit through the entire service with the man glaring at him. Wasn't church about forgiveness and love? Maybe Sam needed to be here as much as he did, Jeremy decided.

Although this was a new experience for him, some of the songs were classics that even a non-church goer knew. Sitting through the service, a calm that he'd never experienced before settled over him. This was one more thing that had been missing in his life. It was something he didn't understand but he knew he wanted it for himself.

Sitting beside Jeremy, Bailey could feel Sam's glare from across the sanctuary. They had been friends most of their lives. She'd never considered him to be anything more than that. He'd never been pushy about his attentions until now. Did he realize there might be someone else she could easily fall in love with?

The thought brought a smile to her lips. She glanced at Jeremy. He seemed entranced by everything around them. Would there even be time to know if he could be the one for her? Jeremy hadn't said how long he was staying in Texas. He'd come here to meet another part of his family, not fall in love.

Since that first morning, he'd gone riding with her every day. His riding skills were improving along with her feelings for him. He'd been impressed with the ranch, asking questions about what ranching entailed. Was he being polite, or was he really interested? Was there an ulterior motive behind his questions? She didn't want that to be true. She wanted him to be as honest and open as he appeared.

From everything she'd heard, Jeremy's great-grandfather expected him to take over the business someday. If that was the case, he would be going back to Kansas, and she would be in Texas.

Pushing these thoughts aside, she tried to focus on the service. The old hymns being sung were her favorites. She knew each of them by heart. The words touched her heart, bringing tears to her eyes as she sang. Glancing at Jeremy, she was surprised to see that he was singing along as well. If she wasn't mistaken, his eyes were a little glassy with unshed tears.

It was one more thing about him that touched her heart. Was it possible to fall in love in such a short amount of time? But what if he went back to Kansas? Where would that leave her? Her place was in Texas. This was her home. She was meant to be a rancher, not the wife of some businessman. A heavy sigh escaped her lips.

Other people moved from the home they'd known all their life to make a new life somewhere else. Parker had done that very thing, leaving Arizona for something entirely different in Iowa? If she'd been afraid to take that leap, she and Shep never would have met. She sighed again. Life could be very complicated.

Maybe she hadn't quite figured out what she wanted to do with her life yet, but there was one thing she knew. She wasn't leaving Promise to live somewhere else. Three of her brothers were happy living in other places, doing other things. But that wasn't for her or Jordan. Ranching was in their blood. Neither of them was going anywhere.

~~~

"Hello, Sam." Kylie stepped up to him as he walked out of the small church. "Mrs. Weston, it's nice to see you."

"Hello, Kylie," Sue Ann's voice was tight. She didn't approve of the young girl. To her way of thinking the girl was much too forward. "I didn't see you inside."

"Oh, I didn't go to church." She gave a little laugh. "I just thought maybe Sam and I could have coffee or something. It was nice seeing him at the bar-b-que. We have a lot in common so maybe we can hang out sometime." She linked her arm through Sam's.

"You were invited to the bar-b-que?" Sue Ann was surprised. She hadn't seen the girl, but with the crush of people that wasn't surprising.

Oh, I wasn't invited," Kylie laughed. "I went anyway. I

wanted to see what all the fuss was about." She shrugged. "It was okay if you like watching your food cook on a spit." She turned to Sam. "I'm hungry. How does lunch sound?"

"Um, I can't. I came with my mom."

"That's all right." She shrugged. "I can drop you off at your place later." It sounded like she dared him to turn her down.

Sam looked across the parking lot where Bailey was getting into the big SUV. She didn't even give him a second glance. "Sure, why not." He looked at his mom. "Kylie will bring me home later." He placed a soft kiss on her cheek. He didn't think she was happy about his decision, but he was a grown man. He didn't need her approval to go out with Kylie. Besides, it would be interesting to find out what she wanted. She always had an agenda for everything she did.

Sue Ann watched as Sam got into the fancy car with that girl. Why was he taking up with the likes of her? She might be the daughter of her husband's 'business partner,' but Sue Ann still didn't like her. Turning away, she was in time to see Bailey Baker in the big SUV with that new guy. Sam should be with her, not that hussy. She shrugged. Things will work themselves out. They always do.

The Fallons all piled into their trucks. They think they are better than everyone else. It is time for a little payback. It's too bad that prick, Davis Fallon isn't here to see his son pay for what he'd done to me.

After church Jeremy helped Dan and Jordan out in the barn. Shep was sitting on a bale of hay. He might not be able to work until his shoulder was healed, but he could still be in the barn with the others. Watching Jeremy, a small grin tilted his lips. He didn't seem to mind helping out around the ranch. Jacob Fallon was going to have a tough time getting Jeremy back in the office after being on the ranch. It was like ranching, or farm work was in his blood.

His great-grandfather said there was too much of Barnard in Jeremy, and Shep thought that might be true. But was he tough enough to stand up to the older man when it came to taking over Fallon Industries? He certainly hoped so. It was plain to him that Bailey had already fallen in love with Jeremy. He didn't want her heart broken if Jeremy knuckled under his great-grandfather's demands.

"I hope these guys aren't giving you all the dirty work." Bailey stepped into the barn. She'd been in the kitchen helping with dinner preparations until her mom chased her out. She was more hindrance than help. Stepping close enough to feel the warmth emanating from his body, she smiled up at him.

"I don't mind." The perfume she wore still lingered in her hair. It had filled the cab of the truck that morning, and he couldn't get it out of his head. "I'd rather be doing something physical than sitting back while other people worked." He knew those words were true. He would never be happy in the office the way his great-grandfather wanted. That wasn't for him. He could still work for the company, just not run it.

He turned his mind to the woman in front of him. He'd deal with his great-grandparents when he returned to Kansas. *If I return,* the thought nearly knocked him off his feet.

"Are you okay?" Bailey touched his arm when he swayed slightly.

He chuckled. "Yeah, I'm fine. I just didn't know that a thought could make your head swim." Until he could examine that thought he couldn't explain it to anyone else. When he came to Texas, he'd had every intention of returning to Kansas and doing battle with Jacob there. Maybe it would be more effective if he took his stand here, where he wanted to be. He knew more than ever that he wasn't cut out to take over from Jacob.

Shep watched from the dimness of the barn with a grin on his face. Yep, there was love in the air. It was like a repeat of him and Parker. From the first moment he'd seen her, he knew she was the one for him. He knew she had felt the same way.

The dinner bell on the front porch rang calling them in to eat. It was an old fashioned system that Bailey loved. She didn't want anything about this place, this town, to change. As long as Jeremy was in Texas, she was going to enjoy his company and let the chips fall where they may.

~~~

With the last of the dinner dishes in the dishwasher, Parker headed for the front porch. The temperature was just right for sitting outside. Wrapping her arms around her middle, she could hardly contain her excitement. Her family would be there the following day.

She was excited to see her folks and brothers. The last time they were all together, she thought that maybe Justin was sweet on Bailey. How would he take the growing attraction between Bailey and Jeremy? She didn't want his heart to be broken.

It was hard being so far away from her family. She loved being with her grandparents in Iowa, but she missed her parents and brothers. For now, she and Shep could pick up and visit with both sides of their family during the winter.

But Shep's business was growing. It wouldn't be long before he couldn't leave in the winter. It would be unfair to make him move his business to either Arizona or Texas and start over again. It looked like Iowa was where they were meant to be, for a while at least.

There were worse things than raising a family on a farm. She'd come to love so many of the people in Whitehaven. She didn't want to leave them either. She sighed. Thoughts of ever selling the house ripped at her heart. Rosie had meant that for her and Shep. It's where everything had started for them.

They had talked about turning the house and barn into a bed and breakfast someday. That was a big undertaking. Was she up to doing something like that? She would have her hands full with a new baby for now. There would be others in the years to come. A bed and breakfast was far down the road for them.

Something her dad had told her once when she started making big plans for her future came to mind. "The way to make God laugh is to tell Him your plans." It wasn't our plans that worked out. It was what God had planned for us. As long as we left Him in charge of our lives, everything came out just the way it was meant to be. A smile lifted her lips. In the end, she was sure that Rosie had seen God's hand in her life.

She looked across the field where Bailey and Jeremy were riding. Bailey loved to ride as much as Shep did. She was glad that Jeremy was interested in learning. The horses were close together; their riders bent almost close enough for them to touch. She smiled at her fanciful thought. If they were meant to be together, nothing anyone did would change that. God was in charge. She sighed happily.

CHAPTER ELEVEN

"Wearin' a path on the porch isn't goin' to get your folks here any faster," Shep drawled, chuckling softly. She'd been pacing ever since Laura called to tell them they were at the airport. As soon as they picked up the rental car, they would be on the way to the ranch.

"I wish they had let me meet them at the airport." She'd said the same thing when Jeremy insisted on renting a car for himself. She rested her head against Shep's broad chest when he pulled her into his arms. His shoulder was healing, but it had only been a few days since he was shot. She was cautious not to disturb the bandage.

"They wanted to have their own transportation so they didn't have to rely on anyone here to take them back and forth to town. If they decide to stay in town instead of here at the ranch, they'll need a car."

"I know," she pouted. It didn't help that he was being so reasonable when she was ready to jump out of her skin with excitement. "It's been over an hour since Mom called." Her voice was muffled against his chest. "What if something happened on their way here? What if…" He tipped her chin up, kissing her to stop the 'what ifs'.

Loud honking broke them apart when a car pulled into the lane. "It's them. Oh, my gosh, they're here." She was bouncing up and down like a bunny rabbit on speed. The waterworks started as soon as she saw her mother's face.

Laura was out of the car before it came to a complete stop. The twins weren't far behind. Laura covered her mouth with her hands, her eyes sparkling with unshed tears. "My baby is having a baby."

Parker's face heated up. She'd always hated when her mom said she was her baby. Now that she was having a baby of her own she understood that sentiment. No matter how old this child was, he or she would always be her baby.

Ben wrapped his wife, daughter, and sons in his strong arms when he made it out of the car.

The rest of the Baker clan poured out onto the porch, joining in hugs all around. "By the way they're carrying on, you'd think it's been years instead of months since they saw each other." Parker's dad chuckled, shaking his head. This was the reason he loved them so much. He was a very lucky man.

Laura pulled Parker back, examining her daughter again. "I can't believe my baby is going to have a baby." Unshed tears shimmered in her eyes.

Noticing the sling on Shep's arm, her tears spilled over. "Are you okay? What did the doctor say about your shoulder?" She wanted to hug him but was afraid of hurting him.

"I'm gonna be fine. It was a through-and-through shot, nothin' vital was hit. By the time we get back to Whitehaven, I'll be as good as new."

"Has the sheriff found the person that shot you?" Ben asked, a worried frown creasing his forehead.

Shep shook his head. "It was probably, a…"

"Don't even say it was a hunter," Parker cut in. "No one believes that."

Shep chuckled. When he started to shrug his shoulders, he winced slightly. "I can't pull anything over on her, not even to keep her from worrying." Pulling her close with his good arm, he placed a kiss on the top of her head.

Ben shook his head. "Don't underestimate her. She's a lot stronger than you think."

Mona led the clan into the house offering iced tea, coffee, and cookies she and her mother-in-law had baked that morning.

Sitting around the fireplace in the great room, Laura looked at Jeremy. "I'm so glad you came for the holidays," she told him. "It means a lot to all of us." Even though he wasn't technically related to Laura through Barnard, she still felt a kinship with him. The term 'love of your life' has been bantered around a lot in recent years. But in the case of Rosie and Barnard, that's exactly what they were. Rosie hadn't loved anyone but Barnard.

"Thank you. That means a lot to me. I just wish I knew more about Barnard to tell everyone." He'd already told the Bakers everything he'd learned about his distant relative since being in Iowa. "Considering the circumstances surrounding Barnard's departure from Kansas, my great-grandparents haven't been very forthcoming with information, and I'm sorry about that."

Jeremy was only distantly related to Barnard, but there was little doubt that he had Barnard's blood. He and Shep looked enough alike they could be brothers. If Barnard had lived, where would this family be today? Laura could see God's hand in all that had happened so long ago. Evil didn't stand a chance against God. He is always in charge.

She reached out to pat his arm. "Everyone is interested in learning about Barnard, but he isn't the reason we're all glad you're here. We want to know you as well."

A warm feeling crept over him at her words. The love everyone had shown him since he arrived was almost overpowering. His great-grandparents weren't the warm fuzzy type. He knew they loved him, but putting that into words wasn't their style.

"I don't have much of a family." He looked at the people around the room. "This many people all at once is a little overwhelming, but everyone has been very welcoming." A smile lit up his face when he looked at Bailey. He felt like he'd spent his life waiting to meet her. It might have been a little over a week since they met, but it felt like he'd known her all his life.

Unable to look away from the expression in his eyes, a soft blush crept over Bailey's cheeks. *How had things happened so quickly?* she wondered. She just met him, but it felt like they'd known each other forever. Without knowing it, her thoughts echoed Jeremy's. She always thought love at first sight only happened in books and movies. Until now, that is.

"Earth to Bailey." Shep snapped his fingers in front of her eyes.

Jerked out of her reverie, she frowned at her brother. "What?"

"Nothin'." There was an innocent expression on his handsome face. "I thought you'd drifted off for a minute." He wrapped his arm around her neck to pull her close. "You're wearin' your heart out there for everyone to see," he whispered in her ear. "You might want to play a little hard to get."

"Yeah, like you did?" she shot back. She didn't bother to keep her voice down. "You told dad you'd met the woman you were gonna marry right after you met Parker."

He looked at his wife sitting beside him, a silly grin on his face. "Yeah, I did." He winced at the pain when he tried to pull Parker to his side with his injured arm. "It just felt right." He shrugged. "I couldn't let her get away." He settled for placing a kiss on her temple.

Mona turned to Laura. "I wish y'all would reconsider about stayin' here. There's no sense of havin' to drive into town only to turn around and come back to the ranch. There's an empty bedroom upstairs, and the den converts into a bedroom where the twins can stay."

"Can't we stay in the bunkhouse?" Justin asked. "We stayed there last summer." Both boys gave their father pleading looks.

"All right," he easily gave in. "I know Laura wants to be close to Parker." He'd anticipated this would happen and had held off making hotel reservations until they arrived.

"I'm so happy for you and Shep," Laura hugged Parker. They were finally alone for a few minutes. She was glad they'd agreed to stay at the ranch. She wouldn't be spending half her time driving to and from town this way.

"Tell me about the twins," Laura said. "I can't wait to see

them. How's Betty doing?"

Parker laughed. "She's fine. Uncle Charlie is still walking on a cloud. Grandpa grumbles about all the time he spends helping Betty out instead of being at the farm with him. But of course, he dotes on them every chance he gets." Thinking about her gruff grandpa with Lillirose and Charlie Junior, she chuckled. They were already calling him CJ.

After all the family had learned about the past and what his grandpa had done to Rosie, her uncle had wanted to honor her in some way. She thought Lillirose did exactly that.

Taking her cell phone out of her pocket, she pulled up her photo gallery. "I took these the day before we left to come to Texas. Just two months old and they're already getting so big." Thinking of her own baby growing inside her, she placed her hand over the baby bump on the belly.

Laura placed her hand over her daughter's. "I can't wait to see them, but I can't wait for my first grandchild even more." Happy tears sparkled in her eyes.

"Oh, don't get me started," Parker laughed, dabbing at her eyes. "It seems like every time I turn around, I'm crying about something that normally wouldn't bother me."

"Those emotional ups and downs were a long time ago for me," Laura said, "but I remember them well. I wanted to share my joy with my mother while I was pregnant with you." She shook her head sadly. "At that time, I knew Daddy wouldn't let her talk to me. By the time I was pregnant with the twins, the lines of communication with them had been closed down completely."

Parker hugged her mom. That had been a hard time for her mom. She wished Grandpa hadn't been so hard. Things were better now. He'd even asked Laura to forgive him. She knew he regretted how he'd treated his only daughter.

Laura brushed away the tears. "That's all in the past. I don't want to dwell on it. If they'd had a cell phone, I could have called Mom direct, but that was long before cell phones were as common as they are now. Besides, I can't see either of my parents with a cell phone." The thought of her stubborn father with a smartphone caused her to chuckle. He resisted change of any kind.

Parker nodded. "Sometimes they seem stuck in the long ago past. But they've come a long way since I moved there. Grandma is more up to date than Grandpa. It helps that Effie and Mable have both embraced technology." She laughed again. "Mable's granddaughter, Caroline, has her set up with a smartphone and a laptop. She even has her own Facebook page. That way she can see her granddaughter's baby in California."

"I was hoping Mom and Daddy would come here for Christmas, but I know they wanted to be there for the twins' first Christmas." She sounded a little sad even though she understood.

"Me, too." Parker nodded. Her eyes began to swim with tears again. "I wish we lived closer to you and Dad. Will you be there when our baby is born?"

"Just try keeping me away," she laughed. "I wouldn't miss it for the world. We'll be there for next Christmas, too. Maybe Shep's parents and grandparents will come, too." As a tear leaked out of the corner of her eye, she changed the subject. "How is Caroline doing on the farm? Do you think she'll be able to make a go of it?"

Parker nodded her head, glad for the change. "She's got a good head on her shoulders and a strong business plan. She already has a small herd of goats along with several cows and a flock of chickens. She's selling eggs and goat's milk. She's even starting her own line of lotions and soap made from goat's milk." She gave a little chuckle. "She's very ambitious."

Laura frowned. "I hope not so ambitious that she fails because she's trying to do everything at once."

"No." Parker shook her head, her red curls bouncing around her face. "As I said, she's smart. Eventually, she wants to raise alpacas. That's just in the research stage right now."

"Alpacas?" Laura laughed. "That girl really is ambitious. I'll bet Mable enjoys having her there."

Parker nodded again. "She has missed so much of her grandchildren's lives. Having Caroline there has been good for her. It's a shame that she let Ed Bodeen convince her to sell the farm in the first place. Did you know Rosie offered to buy her place? Bodeen told Mable that Rosie was trying to cheat her when that was his plan all along. That man was purely evil." A shudder racked her body as she remembered the many things the man had done when she first moved to Whitehaven.

"What do Caroline's parents think of the arrangement?"

Parker shrugged. "At first they were upset with Mable and me for encouraging Caroline. They were certain she was going to fail. She's since managed to convince them she knows what she's doing. They're even planning on spending Christmas with them at the farm. I think it will be the first time they've been there in several years."

She shook her head, setting the curls bouncing again. "I don't know what it is about Iowa that makes some people think they can run their children's lives. Why wouldn't they visit Mable? She's their mother." Emotions got the best of her for a moment, and tears threatened to spill over again. With a frustrated sigh, she swiped at her eyes before any tears could escape. "She was very lonesome before Shep moved in next to her."

Bailey had talked the twins and Jeremy into going for a ride with her after dinner. Parker noticed it hadn't taken much arm twisting to get any of them to agree. The riding skills of all three men were improving. Everyone came outside when they rode up the lane putting an end to the mother-daughter moment. Parker didn't mind. She was going to have her parents for almost a month when they all went back to Iowa after Christmas.

~~~

"My daughter didn't come home for the last two nights," Roger Turner paced around the sheriff's small office. "I want you to find her." He glared at Jose.

"And you're just now getting' 'round to reportin' this?" the sheriff frowned at the man. "Is this somethin' she's done before?" When a young woman disappears there could be any number of reasons.

"Just what are you implying?" Turner stood in front of the sheriff's desk with his feet braced apart and his fists on his hips.

"I'm not implyin' anythin'. I just asked if she's done this before. Maybe she stayed over with a friend. Does she have a boyfriend?"

"No, she doesn't have a boyfriend," he sneered. "Even if she did, what does that have to do with anything? She doesn't sleep around. She wouldn't spend the night with him."

Jose raised an eyebrow but didn't argue. The man was distraught. Young people thought nothing of sleeping with multiple partners before they got married. But Turner was right; he didn't think Kylie Turner had many friends in Promise. "Is it possible she decided to go to Dallas to visit friends?" He tried to be as diplomatic as possible.

"No, she wouldn't do that without telling me. Besides, I've already called one of her girlfriends in Dallas. She hasn't seen her." His stomach rolled. He wasn't much of a father, but he didn't want something bad happening to Kylie. When a young woman disappears without a trace it doesn't turn out very well for the woman.

"When was the last time you saw her?"

Turner had to think before answering. He'd been so caught up in getting this development off the ground he hadn't paid much attention to Kylie. He shrugged. "I had some clients over this weekend to take a look at the plans for the resort. She was supposed to be there to show their son around." His jaw tightened. She'd blown him off. Again. She wasn't any happier about his resort than some of the ranchers.

"But she wasn't there?" Jose asked mildly. How angry had that made Turner? He didn't want to believe a dad would harm his daughter because she wouldn't help him sell some property. But stranger things have happened.

Turner shook his head. He'd had to show the son around the stables on his own. It hadn't been pretty. At least the horse was in the pasture and the man he hired to clean up after the horse had done his job. He was waiting to hear whether the couple decided to buy.

"When was this?" Jose asked.

It was Tuesday morning. Had he been showing the people around on Saturday or Sunday? "I guess it was Saturday," Turner answered his question.

"And you haven't seen her since?" Turner shook his head. "Do you know if she came home Saturday night?" Jose frowned. Kylie could be difficult. She'd raised a ruckus when they first moved to Promise. Would she go somewhere to punish her father?

"I suppose she was there Saturday night," he said defensively. "She's an adult. I don't check on her before going to bed.

"So, it's been more than three days since you saw her, and you're just now reportin' it." The man had no idea how to be a good father.

Kylie had been outside the church Sunday morning talking to Sam Weston. Had she gone off with him?

Sam was generally a good kid, but he'd been upset when his dad sold off part of their ranch to Turner. Would he do something to Kylie as revenge against his dad and Turner? He'd seen so much bad that people do to each other, he tended to see the bad in everyone.

Jose shook his head. He didn't have much respect for the guy before. Now he'd slipped another rung down that ladder. "Have you tried calling her cell phone?"

Turner nodded. "She doesn't answer. I've left several messages, but she hasn't returned my calls. Does that mean something bad has happened to her?" He started wringing his hands.

"It could mean any number of things," Jose answered. "I'll ask around. If you hear from her, call me immediately."

Turner hesitated. "Do you think something awful has happened to her?" he asked again.

The sheriff shrugged. "I won't know that until I investigate. I'll need the names of her friends in Dallas. You can leave that with the sergeant out front. Maybe she called one of them."

"Um, I don't have those names with me. I'll have to give you a call later." He was reluctant to admit that he only knew a handful of her friends in Dallas. He and Kylie hadn't been close before her mom died. It only got worse afterward.

Jose found Elliott in the same place he'd seen him the day after Thanksgiving. Didn't the man ever do any work?

"Twice in one week," Elliott said when Jose got out of his county-issued SUV. "What is it this time? I don't think the kid has gone anywhere today, so you didn't catch him speedin'."

"I just have a few questions. You mind callin' him for me?"

Elliott didn't bother to get up. Instead, he yelled loud enough to raise the dead. "Get your ass down here, Sam. The sheriff wants to talk to you."

Sue Ann came out on the porch. "Is everything okay, Sheriff?" Her hands shook slightly when she brushed her faded brown hair away from her face.

Before he could answer Sam pushed open the door, stepping out onto the porch. "Is something wrong?" He tried to think of a reason the sheriff would need to talk to him.

"Could we talk somewhere privately?" He motioned over by his SUV.

"Whatever you got to say to my son, you can say in front of his mother and me." Elliott sat up straighter in his chair.

Jose shrugged. If that's the way they wanted to play this, it was fine with him. "When was the last time you saw Kylie Turner?"

"Sounds like a trick question, son," Elliott said. "Don't

answer that."

Sam frowned at his dad. "I don't have anything to hide. I haven't done anything wrong." Looking at the sheriff again, he answered the question. "She was waiting outside the church when we came out Sunday. She wanted to go for lunch."

"Is she your girlfriend?"

"Don't answer…"

"Shut up, Dad," Sam snapped. "I told you I haven't done anythin' wrong. No, she isn't my girlfriend. I guess she was lonesome and wanted someone to have lunch with. She doesn't have many friends here in Promise."

"You were with her at the Baker's bar-b-que on Thanksgiving," the sheriff said. He waited to see what Sam would say about that.

"You were with her then?" Elliott said. "What the hell were you doin' with her? I didn't think Baker invited the Turners."

Sam shrugged. "She crashed the party. I was just talkin' with her. I don't think she stayed very long."

"Sheriff, what's this about?" Sue Ann asked softly. "Did something happen to Kylie?"

"Did you drive or did she?" The sheriff ignored Sue Ann's question.

"I went to church with mom. I didn't have my truck. Kylie drove."

"How did you get home?" Pink tinted Sam's face when he admitted Kylie drove him home. "What time did she drop you off?"

Sam shrugged. "Somewhere around one or two, I guess. I didn't look at my watch. What's this about?" He had a bad feeling.

"That's what I'm trying to figure out. Her dad said she hasn't come home for the last few nights." He watched Sam's reaction. "Did she say anythin' about goin' somewhere?" Sam shook his head. "What did you talk about?"

Sam shrugged. "It was kinda strange because she didn't

say much. After we finished eatin', we drove past the house her old man was trying to sell to some big wig from California."

"Hey, her old man ain't the only one involved with that," Elliott objected. "My name's on that resort, too."

"Then why don't you get your ass out there doin' somethin' instead of sittin' around here all the time." Sam had had it with his lazy father.

Elliott came out of the chair like he'd been shot out of a cannon. "You got no right talkin' back to me like that."

Sue Ann stepped in front of her husband. She had to tilt her head back to look him in the face. Her words were so quiet Jose couldn't hear them, but whatever it was sent Elliott back to his chair. "I'm sorry about that, Sheriff. I know you need to ask these questions, but Sam didn't have anythin' to do with that girl gone missin'."

This was all pretty interesting, but Weston's family problems didn't have anything to do with Kylie. Did it? Sam wasn't happy about the resort, Kylie wasn't happy about living in Promise. Had they cooked somethin' up together to get back at their fathers?

"What about that house?" Jose prompted once Elliott had settled down again.

Sam shrugged. "Kylie hopes every one of them burns to the ground. She hates her father for movin' them here."

Elliott gasped, jumping out of the chair again. "She's the one causing all the trouble 'round here lately." One sharp look from his wife and he flopped back down. "You gotta stop her, Sheriff. She's gonna ruin things for me, for us," he quickly added.

Jose ignored Elliott's outburst. "Did she say anythin' else?"

Sam shook his head. "As I said, the whole thing was kinda weird. She just drove around for a while after that. I think she even forgot I was with her. Then she dropped me off here. I haven't seen her since."

The sheriff didn't say anything for several beats before nodding his head. "If you think of anythin', give me a call." He got back in his SUV and drove off. Unless he was reading Sam all wrong, the boy was telling the truth. He didn't have anything to do with Kylie's disappearance. It had been two days since anyone had seen her. She could be anywhere, anything could have happened to her. He needed to get out ahead of this. *If it isn't already too late*, he qualified. His stomach rolled at that thought.

Between Promise and the next town, there was a lot of open range. Part of that was state or federally owned with forests, hills, and even a few lakes or marshland. All in all, there was a lot of ground to cover. If someone wanted to dump a body no one would find, Texas was the place.

That night, Jose stood beside Roger Turner in front of a microphone and camera asking for help finding Kylie Turner. A picture of the young woman was shown. "If anyone has any information on the whereabouts of Kylie, please call the number on the screen."

In most cases where young women have gone missing, parents or close friends plead for the safe return of their loved one. Roger Turner stood in stunned silence. He looked like a beaten man.

Jose had been to all the ranchers asking them to keep an eye out for any sign of foul play.

"I can't believe somethin' like this happened here," Lena said as they all stared at the television. "This isn't the big city."

"Small towns are no longer immune to violence, Grams," Bailey said.

Parker nodded in agreement. Whitehaven was a prime example of that. In the three years since she moved to Iowa, there had been several murders. Even drugs had infiltrated their small town.

"We'll go out at first light tomorrow, searching in quadrants." Dan looked at Shep. "You can coordinate the search from here."

"I should be out there helpin' search," Shep groused. The stitches were due to come out of his shoulder in a couple of days. Until then, the doctor had said no riding. The two Baker ranches alone covered over a thousand acres. They were going to need all the help they could get to cover that much territory.

"In due time," Dan told him. "Until the sheriff gets this figured out no one goes out alone." He gave Bailey a pointed look.

"I don't have to stay behind just because I'm a woman," she stated heatedly. "I'm goin' out to search."

Dan wanted to argue but knew she was right. Bailey knew both ranches like the back of her hand. There were desolate areas, but she had explored every inch of the ranches more than once. She could probably lead her own search party without a problem. That wasn't going to happen though. She would be with him, Jordan, or Shep once he was cleared to ride.

The temperature the next morning was mild enough for Parker to go for a run. The doctor said as long as she didn't overdo it, she could continue running for another month or so. The baby would be fine. Gus wouldn't let anyone get close to her. Shep insisted she run in the field next to the house where he could keep an eye on them.

After a half-hour of dodging cow patties and horse piles, she gave up. It was like running an obstacle course. If you missed one of the obstacles, you had a mess to clean off your shoes. Jogging up the porch steps, she flopped down on the swing.

With a contented sigh, she pushed off with her toe to set the swing in motion. Gus echoed her sigh when he flopped down beside her. His tongue lolled out in a happy grin. Closing her eyes, she said a prayer for the young woman's safety. Something told her it was already too late.

Someone speaking close by woke her with a jerk. Looking

around in alarm, she tried to figure out who was talking to her. Realizing she'd dozed off, she giggled. Never before had she been able to sleep during the day. Now she was either too tired to move, or so energized that she couldn't sit still. It was just one of the many changes she was experiencing.

The voice faded away then came closer to the porch as the speaker paced alongside the house. Realizing Jeremy was talking to someone on the phone, she started to get up to give him some privacy. She didn't want him to think she was eavesdropping. The swing creaked softly, and she stopped.

Looking up at her, he gave a weak smile and turned away. Apparently, he didn't care if she heard his side of the conversation as he continued to argue with whoever was on the other end of the line. He didn't sound happy.

"I'm telling you this is the perfect place to implement my idea," he argued, his words growing softer as he paced away from the porch. There was silence for several moments while he listened to whoever he was talking to.

Parker didn't know what he was talking about, but in the last few years, she'd dealt with some shady characters whose plans would hurt the people she cared about. She'd thought Jeremy was a good guy. Had she been wrong?

Once again he paced toward the front of the house, and she listened hard hoping to figure out who he was talking to. His next words made that clear. "No, I've told you I'm not coming home immediately. I want to stay longer. If you don't think my plan is viable, maybe someone else will."

What kind of plan was he talking about? When they met him over the summer, he had treated his great-grandparents with respect. He was trying to be respectful now, but the older man was making it difficult. Mr. Fallon expected everyone to bend to his wishes. She thought Jeremy had a mind of his own, and was ready to express his wishes even if his great-grandfather didn't like them.

When she heard him again, his voice held barely contained frustration. "I'm no longer a child you can order around." He continued pacing causing his voice to get louder then softer making it difficult for Parker to understand what they were talking about. His frustration had turned to anger when she heard him again. "Yes, I know everything you and Great-grandmother have done for me, but you can't hold that over my head forever. It's time for me to make my own decisions."

Having met the older man, Parker imagined he wasn't used to having people ignore his commands. She silently agreed that it was time for Jeremy to make his own way in the world. She also felt sorry for him. Just because the older couple had raised him, didn't give them the right to dictate what he would do with his life.

"Great-grandfather, please listen to me," Jeremy pleaded. "Kenneth is much more suited to running the company than I am. He's worked for you for years and knows the company inside and out." He was trying to be conciliatory. It wasn't working.

Who is Kenneth? Parker wondered. Obviously, Mr. Fallon wasn't buying Jeremy's argument. He didn't want anyone running his company but Jeremy. When she heard sharp words coming through the phone, she thought Jeremy had probably held the phone away from his ear.

"I'm not turning my back on you and Great-grandmother," Jeremy finally said. "I have ideas that would be a good fit for Fallon Industries if you would only listen to me. I don't want to be in the office all the time. I'd much rather be working out in the field. I want to prove that I have more behind me than a family name."

As most people wanted to do, he wanted to prove to himself and others that he had what it takes to be successful. Maybe Barnard's father had been like Mr. Fallon, dictating to his son what he could and couldn't do. If that was the case, she could understand why he had left his inheritance in Kansas to set out on his own.

A soft sigh escaped her lips as she said a prayer for guidance when their baby arrived. She wanted to protect him or her, but she also wanted them to be able to stand on their own. It was a parent's job to teach their children to be independent adults.

For several minutes her thoughts were taken up with her baby and what the future held for all of them. When she came back to the present, she could no longer hear Jeremy. Either he had walked away or hung up. Her heart went out to him. What the older man was trying to do to Jeremy was similar to what her grandpa had tried to do to her mom.

She asked God to intervene so there wouldn't be the long rift between Jeremy and his great-grandparents like there had been in her family. Mr. Fallon was in his eighties, he didn't have that many years left. He needed to make amends now before it was too late. Only time would tell.

What idea had Jeremy been talking about? Why wouldn't Mr. Fallon even listen to him? If Jeremy wanted a different role in his great-grandfather's company, that meant he planned on returning to Kansas.

From the way Bailey looked at Jeremy she thought her sister-in-law was more than half in love with him. She didn't want Bailey to get her heart broken if he didn't return her feelings. Parker acknowledged that was something else she had no control over.

Please God, be with this family. Guide Jeremy to stand up for what he wants instead of knuckling under to his great-grandfather. Help Mr. Fallon understand that forcing Jeremy to do something against his will would be wrong. And please, Father, be with Kylie. I pray that she knew you.

Placing her worries in God's hands was the only thing she could do. Standing up, she went inside to search out her husband. Maybe he'd heard something from those searching for Kylie.

CHAPTER TWELVE

He hadn't heard from his great-grandfather in over a week. Seeing his name on caller ID, he had hoped the call would be an olive branch. Instead, it was more of the same: orders to come home and guilt when he refused. It had been inevitable that Jacob and Victoria had heard about the missing woman on the national news. Jacob assumed that gave him the right to order Jeremy to come home.

After their disagreement earlier, he had hoped Jacob realized he was serious. He wasn't going to take over Fallon Industries even if that meant leaving the company altogether. When he tried to explain his idea again, Jacob wasn't interested in listening.

Why did his great-grandfather have to be so stubborn? Why wouldn't he listen to any ideas but his own? If the company didn't change with the times, it would eventually fold. He couldn't rely on old technology to keep up with the world. He isn't the only one who can have good ideas.

Jeremy looked out across the field. If Barnard's father had been anything like Jacob, he could understand why he had left Kansas without looking back.

How can I convince Jacob to let Kenneth take over? He silently questioned. I wouldn't be a good CEO. Running his fingers through his dark hair, he sighed. Convincing the older man of that wasn't going to be easy.

Because Jeremy wanted to go his own way, Jacob saw it as a betrayal. But he wasn't turning his back on them. He just wanted to run his own life. Maybe if he hadn't gone to Iowa last summer, he wouldn't be feeling like life was closing in on him.

That wasn't true either. He'd been feeling restless for several years. Four years at the university had taught him that there was more to life than Fallon Industries. He'd rather be researching new possibilities for the company instead of running it.

It also taught him that he could think for himself. He wasn't a clone of the old man. He didn't need his great-grandfather telling him what to do and think all the time. If Jacob wouldn't listen to him, maybe he should look elsewhere. Texas would be a great place to implement his idea.

He sighed. It wasn't just about the desire to prove himself to everyone. An image of Bailey popped into his mind. She was smart, independent, funny, feisty, not to mention beautiful. There was a mutual attraction, and he wanted to explore that to see where it would go. Jacob and Victoria wouldn't like him seeing her any more than they liked anything else he'd said or done in the past six months. Another sigh escaped his full lips.

Unable to remain in one spot any longer, he went inside to change into his running clothes. Running always helped to clear his mind, and rid himself of frustration. He had wanted to go with the search party, but his riding skills weren't any match for the others. He would be a hindrance instead of a help. Even Jason and Justin were able to keep up with the others and had gone with Dan.

An hour later, he wasn't feeling any better than when he started. His mind was still in turmoil. How was he going to convince Jacob that he wasn't the man to run Fallon Industries?

After a quick shower, he stared at the few clothes he'd brought with him. The least casual items he had were chinos and polo shirts. Victoria had wanted to pick out his wardrobe for the trip. At least he'd prevailed in that endeavor.

"You're a wimp, Jeremy," he chastised himself, speaking to his image in the mirror. The most daring thing he'd ever done was to follow them to Iowa last summer. They certainly hadn't expected him to show up.

Remembering the expression on their faces when he turned up at their hotel, he chuckled. For once in his life, he'd taken initiative. He liked the feeling. Accepting the invitation to visit Shep's family in Texas had been just as daring.

What would Shep have done if he hadn't been there to stop Victoria from asking Shep to sign over any rights to the company? Most likely, he would have kicked her off his property. He needed to be a little more like Shep, he told himself. He needed to stand up for what he wanted instead of letting Jacob and Victoria dictate his every move. He promised himself he'd talk to Dan about his idea at the first opportunity.

Turning his mind back to the clothes in the closet, he shook his head. Next to everyone on the ranch, he was almost in formalwear. They all wore jeans and western shirts. *Maybe it wasn't just ranch wear*, he thought. Even Jason and Justin wore jeans and tee shirts. A smile crooked up the corners of his lips. He was going into town to buy some jeans.

He found three of the Baker women in the kitchen preparing the next meal. There were always a lot of people to feed on a ranch. Mona's only help with cooking and cleaning was her mother-in-law and daughter.

Against the wishes of Jacob and Victoria, he had his own apartment. Still, they expected him to have dinner with them every evening unless he was busy with work. Since they returned from Iowa, he'd been making excuses to avoid that every night ritual. He needed his own space.

Even though only two people were living in the big house, Victoria had a housekeeper and a cook. It never occurred to her to do any of the work herself. He was certain she'd never cooked a meal in her life, certainly not in his life.

"I'm going into town," he announced. "Can I pick up anything for you while I'm there?"

"Thank you, Jeremy, that's kind of you to ask." Mona smiled at him. "But that isn't necessary. I think we have everything under control. The men are going to be tired and hungry when they return from the search. We've been praying they find Kylie safe." A bad feeling in the pit of her stomach said that wasn't going to happen.

"Okay, I'll be back in time for dinner." He rushed out to keep from giving an accounting of why he was going into town. Jacob and Victoria always wanted to know where he was going and why. Mona didn't appear upset that he didn't give a reason for his trip. This was a way of living he could get accustomed to, he decided.

An hour later he left the western wear store in Promise. It had taken him considerably longer to buy a couple of pairs of jeans, a western shirt, two tee shirts, and a pair of boots than he expected. He'd gotten an education on buying jeans. There were slim cut, boot cut, relaxed fit, stonewashed, and several other styles he couldn't remember. Who knew? He chuckled. He had to try everything on to make sure it fit.

The clothes he'd worn in were in a sack along with his shoes, and he was sporting a new pair of jeans, a western shirt, and cowboy boots. The clerk told him that boots aren't like shoes. Until they were broken in, they would slip on his heels. He certainly hoped she knew what she was talking about. He felt like a different person, and he liked the feeling. He even liked the sound of the boots striking the sidewalk.

Shopping for clothes wasn't something he normally did. Even in college, all he needed to do was call the store and whatever he needed was sent to the house or his dorm. They had his size in their computer for everything from underwear to shoes to shirts and pants. From now on he was going to pick out his own clothes.

~~~

Where is Kylie? Roger paced around the living room of his big house. Had she gone back to Dallas? God only knew she'd threatened it often enough. She hated living in Nowhere, Texas, as she called Promise. He'd finally found a few names of friends to give the sheriff. So far, none of them had heard from her.

If this was a stunt to get back at him for moving from Dallas, she was going to be sorry. Once he got this resort up and running, they could go back to Dallas. They would have all the money she could ever hope to spend. Until then, he had to press forward.

But having her picture on national television wasn't good for his business. Another couple had been out to look over the property, but when Kylie's disappearance was on national television, they changed their mind. With two young daughters, they didn't feel it was safe to move into the country. It was one more thing Kylie was going to pay for when they found her.

Looking out the big window all he could see for miles was a whole lot of nothing. He was going stir crazy sitting here waiting for news. The sheriff said to stay close to the phone in case Kylie had been kidnapped and was being held for ransom. If that was what happened, Kylie was as good as dead.

That damn Weston had insisted he pay cash for the property he'd bought. He wouldn't take payments or a mortgage. After building this house, he was almost broke or as broke as he ever wanted to be. The money he got from the two houses he'd managed to sell would only last a short time. He needed to find more buyers.

Pushing aside those thoughts, he grabbed his car keys off the counter. Sitting around waiting for the sheriff to call with news wasn't doing him any good.

Pulling up in front of the big town square, he sat in the car for several minutes. Why was this happening to him? Why would someone kidnap Kylie? If she gave her kidnapper as hard a time as she gave him, she should be back by now. She'd been missing four days with no word from a kidnapper. That had to mean she hadn't been abducted for money.

There were a lot of perverts in this world. His stomach twisted. He didn't want to think about something like that happening to her. They didn't always get along, okay, they rarely got along, but he didn't want anything bad to happen to her. How would that look to potential clients? If she'd disappeared on her own as revenge for moving them here, he'd kill her himself.

Getting out of the car, he slammed the door. She was just selfish enough to do something like that. He hoped the sheriff found her, so he could give her a piece of his mind for pulling this little stunt. He had convinced himself that's all this was a stunt to get back at him.

Preoccupied with his angry thoughts, he didn't notice the tall man stepping out of the western wear store. The collision knocked several of the packages the man had been carrying out of his hands.

"Oh! Sorry. I wasn't watching where I was going." He'd been so busy congratulating himself on his purchases, Jeremy hadn't been aware of the man as he stepped up onto the sidewalk.

Ready to berate the man for bumping into him, Roger frowned. He looked vaguely familiar. As the man bent down to pick up his packages, Roger realized why. A big smile spread across his face. "Not your fault," he said, putting all the charm he'd cultivated over the years into his voice. "My wife always said I have tunnel vision when I'm in a hurry." Pretending to be a good ol' boy Texas-style, he stuck out his hand for the younger man to shake.

"Howdy, name's Roger Turner. I'm a real estate developer here in Promise." He chuckled. "Don't you just love that name? It holds out the promise of all the good things available here in Texas." All thoughts of his missing daughter had disappeared from his mind at the thought of a possible client. "Maybe you've seen the signs announcing the development I'm building right here in God's country."

Juggling his packages, Jeremy accepted the man's handshake. "Um, I guess I have." The man was probably talking about those monstrous houses out in the middle of ranch land. "I'm Jeremy Fallon. It's nice to meet you." He tried to step around the man, but Roger was having none of it. The man's name and face seemed vaguely familiar but he didn't remember meeting him before.

"Let me buy you a cup of coffee as an apology for being so clumsy."

"That's not necessary. I wasn't watching where I was going."

"Nonsense. I don't believe I've seen you in town before. You must be new to these parts. Can't let you go thinkin' those of us here in Promise don't have any manners. Where are you from?" Keeping up a steady line of chatter, he swept Jeremy along the sidewalk to the diner.

"I'm from Kansas. I'm here visiting family." Without being rude, there was no way he could avoid the man.

Roger knew exactly who the man was. Over the past year there had been a lot of buzz about Ralph Baker being the illegitimate son of a famous author. He'd never heard of the person, but he'd done some checking anyway. Never let it be said that he didn't do his due diligence when it came to potential clients. Unfortunately, the elder Baker already had a big ranch. He didn't need what Roger was selling.

Turns out, Jeremy Fallon was a shirt-tail relative of the old guy. He was also the heir apparent to the head of some manufacturing company in Kansas. He was just the type of client he was looking for. Once they were seated in the diner, Roger quickly ordered coffee for both of them. "How about a slice of pie? Edna Jean makes the best pies this side of anywhere."

"The name's *Erma* Jean." She pointed to the name stitched on her uniform. "I'm sorry to hear about Kylie." She tried to be sympathetic, but the man didn't make it easy. He was so full of himself it was pitiful. He didn't seem very broken up about his missing daughter.

"Huh?" So focused on his sales pitch that it took a moment to realize what she was talking about. "Oh, thank you." His expression went from eager smiles to sadness in an instant. Jeremy swore there was even a tear in his eye. "Um, could we get two slices of your delicious apple crumb pie along with our coffee?" He waited for her to leave so he could concentrate on Jeremy.

Erma Jean walked off shaking her head. The man didn't give a wit about his daughter. All he cared about was his fancy big development. She hoped it was a big bust.

Jeremy realized where he'd seen the man before. He had been behind the sheriff when he made the plea for any information on the man's missing daughter. He didn't seem broken up that she was missing.

"So, you're from Kansas." He needed to get the guy talking. "What do you do there?" He tried not to be too eager.

Jeremy shrugged. "I work for a manufacturing firm."

"Really? That must be interesting. What kind of products do you manufacture?" He already knew the answer, but asked anyway. Letting on that he knew all about the man would be a mistake.

"Um, farming and mining equipment." Jeremy had come to expect the friendly questions of folks here, but this man's questions were beyond friendly and slipped right into nosy.

"Fallon? As in Fallon Industries?" Over the years, Roger had managed to perfect his innocent expression. "Are you related?"

Erma Jean placed two mugs on the table along with the pie. She cast a sympathetic look in Jeremy's direction before moving off.

"Um, yes, I'm related to that Fallon," he answered. "Distantly related," he added. From past experience he knew to down-play his connection to the family and the company. Some people were a lot more interested in him once they discover who his great-grandfather is. Something told him this guy was one of those people.

"Oh, sure," he realized he was being too pushy and tried to reign in his excitement. "So, how do you like our little corner of heaven? The weather in Texas at this time of year sure beats all that snow Kansas is getting." He gave a hearty laugh. Roger was disappointed when Jeremy nodded without commenting. "How long are you plannin' on bein' in town?"

Talking about the weather was so lame, but he didn't know how to get the guy talking about himself.

"I haven't decided. As I said, I'm visiting relatives."

"Well, if you decide to put down some roots here, maybe you'd be interested in seeing the little development I've got going just outside of Promise. It's f... ah ten sweet acres ready to build your dream house." He was tired of pussyfooting around selling off five acres at a time. Ten acres sound a lot more impressive anyway.

This is the reason he corralled me, Jeremy thought as Turner finally got down to the reason for this impromptu meeting. Was their meeting on the sidewalk as accidental as it first appeared? He shoveled the pie into his mouth swallowing almost before he finished chewing. He wanted to be away from the guy. If his daughter had run off, who was to blame her? He didn't seem concerned that she was missing.

Taking the last bite of pie and finishing his coffee, he casually looked at his watch. "Thank you for the pie and coffee. I spent longer in the store than I realized. I need to head on out before the family sends out a search party. It was nice meeting you, Mr. Turner. I hope they find your daughter" Holding out his hand to the older man, he quickly gathered his packages and walked out.

Roger slumped in the chair. Once again, he hadn't been able to close the sale. Hell, he'd barely been able to make the pitch. If he could have unloaded ten acres, it would tide him over until he could get his hands on other funds.

When Erma Jean placed the ticket on the table beside him, he gave a startled jump. He'd forgotten all about her. "Thanks for coming in, Mr. Turner. I hope you'll be back. Now that you know how good my pies are, you might want to try some of the other items on the menu. I take pride in the food I serve." She was a pretty good saleswoman. "I hope they find Kylie safe and sound." Her tone was sweet enough to decay teeth.

Jeremy didn't breathe until he was safely on the sidewalk

outside. He'd been cornered one too many times by people who either had a bone to pick with his great-grandfather or wanted to sell him something because they thought he had a bundle of money. Mr. Turner fell into the latter category.

People in this town think they are so much better than me, Roger thought angrily. *They need to learn they can't get away with treating me so poorly. They are all going to pay when my development finally takes off. I'll buy this entire town and kick everyone out.* His original plan had been to help the town grow.

At least that's what he told himself. Nothing he ever did was altruistic. There was always an upside for him. He saw nothing wrong with that. Everyone wanted to come out on top. Slapping several bills down, he pushed himself away from the table.

CHAPTER THIRTEEN

On the way back to the ranch, Jeremy's mind raced with the possibilities and opportunities those ten acres Mr. Turner had been pitching could provide. He could set up the wind farm he'd proposed to his great-grandfather. Once that was a reality, maybe he could convince him to begin production on the components for the windmills.

But was the guy legit? His daughter was missing and he was more interested in pitching his resort development than finding her. The man had been pushy, but so were a lot of salesmen. More than that, he'd seemed desperate. Desperate people weren't always honest. Was this some sort of a scam? He didn't even know how much Turner was asking for those ten acres.

Before he did anything, he'd see what Shep and the others had to say about Turner. He already had a pretty good idea what kind of man he was. Maybe pitching his idea to Dan and the others to get their reaction would be best. Not everyone liked the idea of wind farms or windmills.

If Jacob continued to resist Jeremy's idea, he couldn't set up a wind farm on his own. But if he could convince some of the ranchers to set up wind turbines to power their homes it would be a start. He decided to see what Dan and the others thought of the idea.

~~~

Jeremy had gone into town more than two hours ago. She'd been watching for him to return. What was taking him so long? He hadn't said why he was going into town. Of course, he didn't have to explain to her or anyone else what he was doing.

But what if he'd decided he didn't want to stay any longer? Would he just leave without saying good-bye? Her heart ached at the thought. She thought the attraction she felt for him was mutual. Was that all in her imagination? She hoped not. He didn't have any luggage with him when he left, she reminded herself. That must mean he was coming back. Her mind was going in circles.

When his rental car pulled around to the back of the house, the ache in her heart went away at the same time it began beating faster. Stepping out of the barn, she waited for him to get out of the car. The man was really something else. She'd known him less than a month, but the attraction she felt for him was like a magnet. She couldn't seem to get away. And she didn't want to, she admitted to herself. A dreamy smile lit up her face.

When he stepped out of his car, she couldn't help but laugh. "Well, what happened to the city slicker who came here a couple of weeks ago?" She teased as she walked across the yard.

"Why, ma'am," he said, putting on his best imitation of a Texas drawl, "you and this country have transformed me." Truer words had never been spoken. He didn't want the kind of life his great-grandparents led. During his entire life, he couldn't remember any show of affection between them.

He wanted this woman and the life these people could offer. For a long time, he'd felt a restlessness he couldn't explain. Now he knew what it meant. This woman, this place, is where he belonged.

There was still a lot he could offer Fallon Industries, but not as CEO. He had his Engineering Degree and he could help to grow the company. But he would never go back to working solely in an office. Making his great-grandparents understand that wasn't going to be easy, if at all. If they fought him on this, they were the ones to lose. Victoria was very good at laying on the guilt, and Jacob simply walked right over anyone who disagreed with him. Jeremy admitted that he'd let him do that for years. But no more.

Meeting her in the middle of the yard, he resisted the urge to pull her into his arms and kiss her. Instead, he casually draped his arm across her shoulders. Wrapping her arm around his slim waist, she looked up at him. For a minute, he thought his heart would burst. There was a light in her eyes that he couldn't put a name to.

"Well, look at you." Mona smiled at him when they walked into the kitchen. "You're beginning to look like a real Texan, right down to the boots."

"When in Rome," he chuckled, feeling self-conscious at the scrutiny. "Riding a horse in dress pants and dress shoes just didn't seem right somehow."

"Well, you look very nice," Laura said. The women didn't miss the young couple was holding hands.

"Supper will be ready in about an hour. I think you have time to go for a short ride after you drop off your packages. You can test out those new duds."

Bailey's heart was doing flips. She'd been afraid that the attraction she felt was only one-sided. Now they had to figure out whether what they felt was real or simply a flirtation. She pushed aside the fact that he lived in Kansas and she lived in Texas. She didn't want to leave her home and family. Did he feel the same way about Kansas? She sighed. It was something they were going to have to figure out before this went any further.

As much as he wanted to talk to Dan and the others about his idea and Turner, he didn't want to waste the opportunity to be with Bailey. He decided Turner could wait. The guy was scum if he was more interested in a sale than finding his daughter.

Talk around the supper table centered on the upcoming holiday. Everyone was getting excited. The house looked like a fairyland to Jeremy. Nothing like this happened in the big house Jacob and Victoria lived in.

After he'd graduated from college, Jeremy had insisted on having his own place. It hadn't set well with the older couple, but he hadn't backed down. He wasn't going to back down on refusing to become the next CEO at Fallon Industries either. It was a vow he made to himself that he intended to keep.

"There's going to be thirty people here for Christmas dinner?" he whispered to Bailey as they pushed back from the table. He couldn't keep the wonder out of his voice.

Bailey nodded her head. "Jordan's girlfriend is flying in from Austin for the holiday, and Cameron will be here with his fiancé," she explained. "The ranch hands that don't have family close by always join us. Dad's vet assistant and her husband will be here as well."

Looking back at past Christmases with Jacob and Victoria, it had always been just the three of them. He wondered what they would do for Christmas dinner this year with him gone. It probably wouldn't be much different from every other year. Mrs. Lampson would prepare and serve the meal before going home to her family.

It would never occur to the older couple to invite her family to join them. He wasn't even sure if she would accept such an invitation. Their relationship was purely that of employer and employee. Of the few friends his great-grandparents had over the years, not many were left.

This was the first year in his memory that he'd been away from them during any major holiday. Even while he was in college, he had gone home for the holiday. It was sad to think of them all alone, but they'd brought this on themselves. They didn't even bother inviting Kenneth to join them.

Because he was related to Victoria, Jacob didn't consider him family. To him, only someone with Fallon blood was family. That meant Jeremy. As Jacob often reminded him, he was the last of the Fallon line. He tried not to feel guilty for being here.

On a ranch, work didn't stop or slow down because a holiday was coming up. There was even more work to be done. Everyone had jobs to do to get ready for the holiday. Evenings were the time to relax and enjoy those gathered here. Christmas music played softly in the background. Would they have a family singalong on Christmas like they had in some holiday movies? He shook his head at his fanciful thoughts.

He didn't know what to expect, but this was what he wanted, he told himself. The more he thought about it, the property Mr. Turner had tried to sell him wasn't such a bad idea. Of course, he hadn't asked any particulars, like the price.

Before he did anything, he'd ask the family about the man. The family, yes, these people were family. Even those that weren't blood-related were considered family. A smile lifted the corners of his mouth.

"I have a favor to ask." Ralph pulled Parker aside after the dishes were cleared off the table.

"Certainly, I'll do anything I can." She wasn't sure what he was getting at, but it seemed important to him.

"I've been working on Rosie's unfinished manuscript. I'm not sure how I'm doing." He chuckled. "I had to get help putting what Rosie already wrote onto my computer; otherwise I would have to type everything in myself." He sighed at the thought of that daunting task. "Would you read what I have and let me know what you think?"

"I'd love to." She beamed at him. She'd been hoping he would finish it.

"Lena surprised me with a collection of all the stories I told the grandkids as they were growing up." His face turned pink at the mention of those stories. "She said she loved hearing me tell those stories, so she started recording them. I didn't know she was doing that. She finally typed them up after you sent the manuscript.

"She even did a few illustrations to go along with the stories. She thinks they're good enough to be published." He shook his head. "I think she's just sayin' that because she's my wife. She's always supported me in anythin' I wanted to do."

"I'm sure she wasn't saying that just because she's your wife," she assured him. "Shep has told me some of the ones he remembers. I'd love to help you with those as well."

"Could we keep this between the two of us for now?" He looked around to see if any of the others were paying attention to them. "I don't think there's any reason for the others to know about this in case you think I'm being an old fool."

Parker placed a kiss on his cheek. "I don't think you're a fool, old or otherwise." She chuckled. "Shep has very fond memories of hearing those stories. I hope you'll tell them to our baby when he or she is old enough to listen." She rested her hand on her stomach.

Linking her arm through his, they slipped into the great room. Jeremy was telling about his trip to town. "I bumped into Roger Turner while I was there." He chuckled. "I literally bumped into him. Coming out of the store, I wasn't paying attention to where I was going. I almost got knocked over when I ran into him. I know his daughter is the missing girl, but he was telling me about this development he has going. Is it legit?"

An uncomfortable silence filled the air for several moments, and he wondered if he'd said something wrong. He'd gone this far, he kept going. "It was my fault, but he insisted on buying me a cup of coffee and a piece of pie to apologize. He almost dragged me into the diner." He was picking up on some uncomfortable vibes. "Did they find his daughter?"

Dan shook his head. "No, she's still missin'. There's a lot of ground to cover if she's even still in the area. Did he try to sell you one of his mini ranches?" Dan asked with a frown. It wasn't exactly an answer to Jeremy's question.

"Um, yeah. I thought it was strange that he was trying to sell me ten acres in this development while his daughter was missing. It was like he didn't even care about her."

"He probably doesn't," Bailey muttered.

"Ten acres?" Dan asked.

Jeremy nodded. "Why? Is there something wrong with that?"

"No. Until now he's been hoping to sell five-acres at a time," Dan said. "It sounds like he's upping his game. What did you tell him?"

"Nothing." Jeremy shook his head. "I got out of there as fast as I could. I said I was running late, and I needed to head back to the ranch. He seemed a little too... eager. I figured he knows who I am and that I'm related to you all."

"I don't know why he tried to sell you on his big development," Dan said.

Jeremy shrugged. "It wouldn't be the first time someone found out who my great-grandparents are and tried to hit me up for money. I've seen a couple of big houses between here and town. Are those part of his development?"

Dan nodded. "Weston sold him half of his ranch to start this big resort he keeps talkin' about." He sighed. "Even at ten acres each, that's a lot of houses goin' up. Not many of the other ranchers are happy about it." He paused. "Are you interested in one of those houses?" A frown drew his dark brows into a V over his eyes.

"Um, I'm not real sure. I didn't come here looking to stay forever, but..." He cast a furtive glance at Bailey. "I've sort of got this idea I've been trying to sell Jacob on, but he isn't interested. This might be a good place for it. Besides, it might be nice to have something to call my own"

If things worked out the way he was beginning to hope, it would be nice to have a place of his own. His eyes drifted to Bailey again. Ten acres wouldn't make for a very big wind farm, but it would be a start. He would be able to show the locals what the possibilities were with wind power.

What would she think of his idea? Some people, including Jacob, thought wind farms were ridiculous. Environmentalists were also against the idea. Windmills killed birds.

"What is the idea you're trying to sell your great-granddad on?" Shep asked. Jeremy struck him as being smart. If he didn't want to follow in Jacob's footsteps, he might be able to start something on his own.

"Oh, um." He felt all eyes on him now. "In college, I did a paper on renewable energy sources. There are a lot of wind farms across the country. A wind farm in the right location can produce enough energy to serve a small town. In some locations where the wind blows most of the time and doesn't have enough sun for solar energy for their homes, people are starting to use wind turbines instead."

"A location like Texas?" Ralph asked. One eyebrow lifted slightly in question.

Jeremy nodded. "Yes, I think wind turbines would be useful here. I know there are already wind farms in different parts of Texas. Wind power could also bring electricity into individual homes." He sighed. "I tried to tell Jacob that Fallon Industries could even begin to manufacture the necessary parts. It wouldn't take much to convert over part of the factory from farm and mine equipment." He shook his head. "Naturally, he wasn't interested."

"There are a lot of wind farms in Iowa," Shep said. "I don't see why it wouldn't work here as well. The wind certainly blows enough." He chuckled. "We might even be able to use one at the farm." He looked at Parker. Her slight nod meant she agreed it was something they should think about.

He could almost read her thoughts behind the smile playing around her lips. This was something their little LLC could get behind. They had helped a lot of people out, so why not Jeremy? It seemed like he'd put a lot of thoughts behind his idea.

Excitement zinged through Jeremy's veins as he got ready for bed later that evening. No one had put down his idea of a wind farm or a wind turbine on individual properties. If Jacob continued to refuse to listen to the idea, he might be able to do it on his own. A company like that would need to start small. That was something he thought he could do.

CHAPTER FOURTEEN

It had been more than two weeks since Kylie went missing. With so much open range, there were still a lot of places to search. When Dan wasn't tied up with his veterinary practice, he was out helping look for her. Without anything new, the case had lost traction on the national news.

Shep's shoulder was healed enough for him to get on a horse. Jordan and Bailey joined him in the search along with their granddad. The longer the search went on, the smaller the search parties became. It was like no one cared any longer, or had given up, even Turner.

It was late in the day when the call came in. "We've found Kylie's body," Jose said. He sounded bone-weary. There hadn't been a murder in his county in more years than he could count. This one wasn't going to be easy.

"Where?" Dan asked, turning to his dad and the others in the search party.

"On the far side of The Red River," Jose said. "There's a shack that's about ready to fall down. She was in there. Wildlife got to her pretty good, but it's her."

Dan sighed. The Red River ran through his parents' ranch. He knew the shack Jose was talking about. It was about a day's ride from the main house. "Any sign of how she got there? Have you located her car?"

"The car was in the river. If this was spring with all the runoff from the snow in the mountain, we wouldn't have seen it. It'll be a few days before the ME can give me cause of death and whether she was killed there or brought there later."

"Have you contacted Turner?"

There was silence for several seconds before Jose answered. "I can usually read a person pretty good, but that's one guy I can't get a read on. I don't know if he's upset, relieved, or angry. Maybe a little of each. I guess people grieve in their own way." He sighed. "I just wanted to let you know so you can call off the search.

"My heart goes out to Roger," Lena said when Dan gave everyone the news when he got home. "He never seemed all that interested in findin' her, but this has to hit him pretty hard. He's lost his wife and now his daughter." She gave her gray head a shake.

"He didn't even join in the search," Jordan said. "Can't say he was much of a father." If this had been one of his kids, Dan wouldn't sleep until they had been found. Instead, Turner went about like it was business as usual.

"Can you really see that man on a horse?" Bailey asked. "He'd hold everyone back."

"Yeah, maybe," Dan said. He had his own thoughts about Turner.

The next morning Jose was at the Baker ranch as they were sitting down to breakfast. "Mornin', Jose." Mona pushed open the back door. "Can I get you a cup of coffee?"

"Thanks, it's been a long night, toppin' off a couple of long weeks." She set a steaming mug on the table in front of him.

"I suppose you've heard what Turner is sayin'." He looked at Dan.

"Yep, Dad just called to let me know you were on your way here. You don't really think any of us had anythin' to do with this."

"I have to follow up on every lead, even if it's false." That wasn't exactly a ringing endorsement that he believed they were innocent.

"Why is Turner sayin' Dad or Granddad had anythin' to do with Kylie's death?" Shep asked.

Jose looked at his friend. "The two of you have spoken the loudest against his development. He said he's more determined than ever to make it happen. He's gonna name it after Kylie."

"It seems like he's thought this out pretty good," Jeremy said. The guy had seemed desperate that day in the diner. How would killing his own daughter help his development? How much life insurance did he have on her? It wasn't something he would suggest to the sheriff, but he hoped the man would check it out.

Jose didn't believe either Dan or Ralph would do something like this, but he still had to take Turner's accusation seriously. It would be pretty stupid of them to leave the girl on their own land if they'd killed her. When he'd suggested that to Turner, he said that was probably what they were thinking. No one would accuse them of leaving the body of someone they'd killed on their land.

The fact that Jeremy's windbreaker had been found under the body seemed a little too obvious as well. It was the only clue they had found at the scene. He didn't think Jeremy was so stupid to fake the theft of his own jacket and leave it with a woman he'd killed. Besides, he had been in the house at the time the car had been broken into. What motive would Jeremy have to kill Kylie? Things weren't adding up.

What did all of these things have in common? It seemed a little too much of a coincidence to have four separate crimes tied to the same family. The only common denominator was the arrival of Jeremy Fallon. Was that another coincidence?

~~~

"If you aren't going to arrest someone for killing my daughter, I'll go over your head. I happen to know the state's Attorney General." Roger Turner paced around the sheriff's small office.

Jose didn't know if that was true, but it didn't make any difference. No one could force him to make an arrest without any evidence. "Mr. Turner, this is still an ongoing investigation. These things take time."

"I don't have time."

Jose frowned. What did that mean? "Is there a reason you're trying to rush me into making an arrest?"

Turner stared at him for a long moment choosing his next words carefully. "I want justice for my daughter," he finally said.

"So do I, but I can't arrest someone without evidence."

"How much more evidence do you need? She was found on the Baker ranch. All of the Bakers have fought against my development since day one." Jose had withheld the fact that Jeremy's jacket was found with the body. If anyone mentioned that, it would point an accusing finger at the killer.

"That doesn't mean they killed your daughter."

"I'll bet if Baker's daughter was killed you wouldn't be sitting on your hands doing nothing."

Jose stood up, glaring at the man. "I suggest you go home before you say something you can't take back." A muscle in Jose's jaw bunched as he tried to keep from physically throwing the man out of his office. He didn't play favorites when it came to solving a crime. "Remember spreading unsubstantiated rumors can also come back to bite you," he warned.

Turner stormed out of the office, slamming the door hard enough to rattle the glass window.

The autopsy report was sitting on his desk. Kylie had been strangled. From the position of the bruises on her neck, her killer was several inches shorter than her. The cord was still wrapped around her neck when she'd been found. There was nothing to distinguish it from any other cord you could buy at the hardware store. The only DNA found on the cord belonged to Kylie. The killer must have worn gloves. There was no sign of sexual assault either.

He'd questioned the Bakers again about possible enemies who would want to throw guilt their way. Asking Jeremy Fallon the same thing hadn't been any more productive. The only person upset with him was Bill Hancock and that still seemed an unlikely reason to kill Kylie. Bill's whereabouts were also unknown. Since he was no longer working for Weston, he might have left Promise looking for work elsewhere.

The time of death wasn't easy to determine after this

length of time. After dropping Sam Weston off the Sunday after Thanksgiving, no one had seen Kylie again.

Questioning Sam again hadn't been productive either. He claimed that going to lunch with her was the closest thing to a date he had with her. Sue Ann seemed more upset by the implication that her son might have been dating Kylie than him being a potential murder suspect. Elliott on the other hand was ready to blame his son for any delays in the resort development. He felt like he was going in circles.

Christmas in Texas was certainly different from Kansas. There was no snow on the ground, and the temperature was a mild sixty degrees. Before the family left for church that morning, Jeremy called his great-grandparents to wish them a Merry Christmas. It was early, but he knew Jacob would be at his desk. It might be a holiday, but he didn't know how to relax. Even though he was in his mid-eighties, his day started before six on any given morning and didn't end until dark. He managed to get by on four or five hours of sleep every night.

"Oh, you finally found time to call your family," the old man barked without any greeting.

Jeremy hadn't expected Jacob to be happy, but he hadn't expected him to be hostile either. "Merry Christmas to you, too, Great-grandfather." He tried to remain cheerful, but it wasn't easy. Had the man always been like this? Why hadn't he seen it before?

"It's not going to be Christmas for your great-grandmother and me with you so far away," Jacob grumbled. "When are you coming home? Work is piling up."

"What work? Kenneth is probably working overtime to do everything you want done."

"Kenneth is no longer with the company."

"What? Why? What happened?"

"He left the company for a better offer."

"He would never leave on his own. Great-grandfather, what did you do?"

"Nothing," he denied.

"I don't believe that. If you fired him because of what I said, you made a big mistake. I have tried to tell you that I don't want to be the CEO. There is nothing you can do or say that will make me change my mind."

"Is it because of those people that you're doing this? Have they turned you against your own family?"

"They haven't done anything. This is all on you. Did you fire Kenneth?"

"I said he got a better offer elsewhere." Jeremy didn't miss the fact that Jacob evaded the question.

"That isn't what I asked. If you fired him because of what I said, you might as well fire me too because I'm not going to be CEO. I can't believe you were this heartless." He paused, waiting to see what Jacob would say. When he remained silent, Jeremy sighed.

"Tell Great-grandmother that I will call her later to wish her a Merry Christmas. When you come to your senses, you can call me. Good-bye." Jeremy ended the call without waiting to see if his great-grandfather would say anything. There'd already been enough said.

Running his long fingers through his hair, he hung his head. How could he do that to Kenneth? What did Victoria have to say about it? Kenneth was her great-nephew. Was she as heartless as her husband? He didn't want to know the answer to that. He always thought they were good people. Now he wasn't so sure.

Parker had shared with him what had happened in her family between her mom and grandfather. After more than twenty-five years, there had been a happy resolution. He didn't think that would happen with him and his great-grandparents.

If Barnard's father was like Jacob, he understood why he'd walked away without looking back. Did he have it in him to do the same thing? He shook his head, not wanting to think about that. They were his great-grandparents and had raised him when his parents hadn't cared enough. Because of that, he loved them, but right now he couldn't say that he liked them. He wouldn't let them run his life. Why couldn't they understand that?

A soft tap on his door brought him out of his morose thoughts. There were happier things to think about. "Merry Christmas, Beautiful." Without thinking, he bent his head, placing a soft kiss on Bailey's lips.

"Wow!" She gave a soft sigh when he lifted his head. "What took you so long?" Her hand slipped around his neck, boldly pulling his head down for another, longer kiss.

At the sound of someone clearing their throat, they jerked apart. Shep and his younger brother Jordan stood across the hall from them. His face flamed hot at being caught kissing their sister. The contrasting expressions on their faces didn't bode well for him. Shep didn't appear to mind, while Jordan was scowling at him.

"Did you need something, guys?" Bailey asked coolly. Her hand rested on Jeremy's chest as she looked over her shoulder at her brothers. She didn't appear the least bit upset at getting caught kissing him.

"Does Dad know about what's going on under his roof?" Jordan asked with the voice of doom.

"What are you implying Dad should know about?" Bailey asked mildly, turning to face her brother. "I'm sure he's aware that I've kissed guys before."

"Standing in the hall outside of your bedroom?" He arched an eyebrow at her.

"Hold on, Jordan." Shep intervened. "If you're suggestin' what I think you're suggestin', you've got this all wrong."

"Shut up, Shep. I don't need you to fight my battles." Bailey marched the few feet separating her from her brothers. Standing toe-to-toe with Jordan, she tipped her head back so she could look him in the eye. She might be petite, but she was mighty. Fire spit from her eyes.

"Get your mind out of the gutter. You sound like someone

with a guilty conscience. You can't blame me for what you've done. We aren't doing anything wrong. What do you think happened that you have to tell Dad?"

Stepping between the siblings, Jeremy didn't give Jordan a chance to answer. "Jordan, if you have a problem with me kissing your sister, I'm sorry about that. As she said, we weren't doing anything wrong. I like her very much, and with or without your permission, I intend to explore what that could mean. When such a time comes that there is something more between us, I'll go to your father, not you, with my intentions. Got that?"

He surprised everyone, including himself, with that little speech. He'd never spoken to anyone in that manner before. But he was tired of people telling him what he was supposed to do and feel.

"She's my little sister, and I'll always want to protect her," Jordan said. All fire had disappeared from his voice. "But I understand what you're sayin'." A crooked smile lifted his lips. He offered his hand to Jeremy.

Jeremy paused several long seconds as he stared eye to eye at Jordan. A silent communication seemed to pass between them, and he took the proffered hand. The awkward moment had passed.

Bailey released the breath she'd been holding. "Men," she muttered, shaking her head. "Always with the pissin' contest. To heck with all of you." She marched off without a backward glance.

"Uh oh, I think someone is in a bushel of trouble now." Shep clasped Jeremy's shoulder. "I hope you know what you're gettin' into with that one. She's a spitfire."

Jeremy made like he was wiping sweat from his brow. "Yeah, she is." A grin split his face as he watched her lope down the stairs. "But I'm up to the challenge. I wouldn't change her for all the money in the world. I like her just the way she is." He turned back to the brothers. "From what little I've heard about Rosie, I think there is some of her in all of your family."

Thinking about his recent conversation with Jacob, he sighed. "I wish there was some of her in me." The upcoming battle with his great-grandfather was going to make what just happened between Bailey and Jordan seem like a minor dispute.

"Whatever is goin' on with you, I think you'll do just fine." Jordan chuckled. "You might not be blood-related to Rosie, but maybe Barnard was just as feisty. After all, he walked away from what could have been his, to find his own way."

"What happened to get your sister's dander up?" Dan met the three men as they entered the kitchen. "It's Christmas, peace on earth and all. She stormed out of here like she was ready to take someone down. Which one of you stepped in it?" He eyed each of them, his head cocked to one side.

"That would be me, Dad." Jordan shook his head. Dan silently waited for his son to explain.

"It's all okay, Sir," Jeremy said. "Where is she? I'll take care of it."

"Where she always goes when she's upset," he said. "She's in the barn talking over what happened with .Windstar." When Jeremy headed for the door, he said: "We leave for church in thirty minutes. If you haven't settled her down by then, we'll leave without her. Seems to me she needs to go more than some others."

"Maybe I'll leave that part out." Jeremy chuckled as he pushed open the door.

Bailey stroked the chestnut mare's side, her face buried in the long mane. "Why do men have to be so stupid?" Tears clogged her throat. "They think they have to take care of everyone. Well, they're wrong. I can take care of myself. I don't need a stupid man to do it for me."

"I'm sorry." Bailey froze. She didn't want him to see her angry tears. "I just thought Jordan needed to know that whatever my intentions are, they're honorable. Next time someone tries to tell you what you can do, I promise I'll try to let you handle it."

"Are you makin' fun of me?" She still didn't turn around. If that was what he was doing, she just might smack him.

"No! Why would you think that?" He was mucking things up further.

Wiping her face with the back of her hand, she finally turned around. Her green eyes were luminous, a single tear balanced on her lashes nearly taking him to his knees. "I don't need someone to fight my battles. I'm a big girl."

"I know you are, and I didn't mean to imply that you can't take care of yourself. I wanted Jordan to know that I would never take advantage of you. I want to get to know you. Do you think we can get past this?"

He paused then held up his hand to stop her from answering right away. "Before you say anything, you need to know that if someone tries to hurt you, I will stop them. Not because I don't think you can take care of yourself, but because I care about you. I don't want anyone to ever hurt you. If that's a bad thing, I'm sorry."

She threw herself at him, nearly taking them both to the straw-covered floor. "I'm sorry," she whispered against his chest. "You have no idea what it's like to have four big brothers always telling me what to do."

"No, I don't have any brothers, or sisters for that matter," he chuckled. "But I do have a great-grandfather who has been controlling my life as far back as I can remember. So I guess we're even on that score. I'll do my best not to step in when it's something you can handle. But remember what I said. No one is going to hurt you unless they go through me first." Putting his finger beneath her chin, he tipped her head up allowing him to place a light kiss on her lips.

He slowly lifted his head when a horn honked out in the yard. "I think your dad is telling us to get a move on or we'll miss church." Taking her hand, they raced out of the barn together.

CHAPTER FIFTEEN

What is that stupid sheriff waiting for? There was enough evidence in that shack to put a noose around Fallon's neck. But of course, he's a Fallon, so he's gonna get a pass. Well, I can't let that happen. He's gonna pay for everything his father did to me. The Bible says the sins of the father will be passed on to the sons even to the seventh generation. Or something like that.

Waiting for that stupid sheriff to get done what needed to get done isn't working. It's time to take things into my own hands. Maybe another murder was what it would take to get the sheriff off the pot. First I'll need something to point that stupid sheriff in the right direction. He can't find his way out of a paper bag.

~~~

"Did you mean what you said this morning?" There were stars in Bailey's eyes when she looked up at Jeremy. He had followed her to the barn after they returned from church. Even on Christmas, the animals needed tending. The ranch hands had the day off, but Windstar was her responsibility. She needed to be fed, and her stall needed to be mucked out. On a ranch, there were always jobs that needed to be done no matter what day it was. Jeremy didn't seem to mind helping her do what most people considered the worst job on the ranch.

"I don't make a habit of saying things I don't mean. I care about you. I know we haven't known each other very long, but in some cases that doesn't matter." Before he could say anything else his phone vibrated in the pocket of the jacket he was wearing. Without his windbreaker, he had borrowed one of Shep's denim jackets.

With a sigh, he pulled it out. His shoulders drooped slightly as he saw who was calling. "I'm sorry. It's my great-grandmother. I haven't called to wish her Merry Christmas. She isn't going to be happy with me." He walked out of the barn before accepting the call.

"Merry Christmas, Great-grandmother."

"I've waited for hours for your call. I thought you probably forgot about me." She was shoveling on the guilt a little heavier than usual.

"No, I didn't forget about you. I've been busy."

"With your new family," she finished the sentence for him.

"People can have more than one family. You and Great-grandfather will always be my family. Just because I like these people doesn't mean I've forgotten you and Great-grandfather." Those titles were becoming a bigger mouthful all the time. He wished he could shorten it to Pops, or Granddad, or simply drop the 'great' part.

"Did Great-grandfather tell you I called earlier? I wanted to talk to you then, but what he told me made it impossible to continue the conversation."

"What did he tell you?" He could picture the frown that drew her eyebrows low over her faded eyes.

"Kenneth is no longer with the company." What would she say to that?

"Yes, he took a position with another company." She parroted what Jacob had said.

"I seriously doubt that was his idea. Kenneth loved Fallon Industries. He's been there since he graduated from college. How could you let Jacob fire him?"

"*Jacob?*" Her voice went shrill. "You're no longer calling us by the titles we've earned? We raised you. How can you turn your back on us?"

"How could you turn your back on Kenneth and let him be fired?" He used her own words on her. "He's your family, too."

She ignored the last part of what he said. "I don't tell your great-grandfather how to run his company. You of all people should know that. Kenneth left of his own accord. He wasn't fired." She paused for a moment before changing the subject. "When are you coming home? You're needed here now that

Kenneth has left."

"I don't know when I'll be back. You both have given me a lot to think about."

"Such as?"

"Such as my future with a company that would fire someone without just cause," he said. He pushed on before she could argue that point. "Such as my future with a company that won't listen to their employees, especially the one employee they claim is the most important one. I have told both of you more times than I can count that I don't want to be CEO. I wouldn't be any good in that position. I've tried to tell Great-grandfather that the job should go to Kenneth. I have ideas I would like to see implemented but he won't listen to that either." He drew a deep breath, releasing it slowly.

She was silent so long he thought the call had been dropped. "Come home and we can talk about your ideas," she finally said.

"Not yet. I hope you and Great-grandfather had a nice Christmas. Call some of your friends and invite them over. Invite Mrs. Lampson's family to dine with you."

"Mrs. Lampson? You mean the cook?" Her voice squeaked at the very idea of inviting the household help to eat with them.

"Yes, the cook," he said with a sigh. "She's cooked your meals for years and you barely know her name. I need to go now. The horses need to be fed. I love you, Great-grandmother. Despite of all that has been said and done, I do love you both." With a heavy heart, he ended the call. They would never accept that he didn't want to run Fallon Industries.

"Is everything all right?" Bailey asked when he went back into the barn. "Do you need to go back to Kansas?"

"No, everything isn't all right. And I don't know if I'd be welcome if I went back." He sighed. "Families aren't easy to deal with sometimes."

He sounded so sad the only thing she could think to do

was to hug him. Wrapping her arms around his waist, she held him close. Comfort quickly heated up, and he pulled her slightly away to look down into those startlingly green eyes. "I think I'm falling in love with you," he whispered. "I hope you don't mind." Lowering his head, he placed his lips against her letting her feel all the emotions he had stored up inside him. They were both breathing heavily when he finally lifted his head.

"I don't mind at all because I love you, too," she whispered when she could catch her breath.

"You don't think it's too soon to know?" He cocked his head to one side.

"We can take as long as you want, but I know what I'm feeling is real. I'm not going to change my mind."

Several cars pulled into the lane. People were beginning to arrive for dinner. The pile of presents that had surrounded the big tree in the great room had been opened the night before. Over the past month, he had bought presents for everyone. While in college, he'd bought presents for his friends, but this was the first time he had a large shopping list to fill. He couldn't imagine ever going back to only having three people around the table on any holiday.

The whole day was magical for Jeremy. Jordan surprised his girlfriend with an engagement ring. Jordan was the serious brother, but suddenly he turned very romantic.

Another surprise had been Dan's vet assistant's announcement that she was pregnant. There was a lot of that going around. Every day he could see the difference in Parker's usually petite figure as her pregnancy developed.

There was another surprise waiting for him the next day when Kenneth showed up at the ranch. "Merry Christmas, Jeremy." He stood on the porch.

"Kenneth?" Jeremy stared at the man as though he was seeing an apparition unable to believe his eyes. "What are you doing here?"

"I needed to see you," Kenneth stated simply.

Stunned, Jeremy wasn't sure how he was to respond to that. "Okay." He stepped out onto the porch. This wasn't his house. He wouldn't invite someone in without checking with Mona or Dan first.

"Why did you come here? Is this because Great-grandfather fired you?" he asked. He couldn't think of any other reason Kenneth would want to talk to him. They worked together and were cousins of some sort, but they didn't hang out together. Kenneth was almost as serious about business as Jacob. That's why he thought Kenneth was the person to succeed him.

"No." Kenneth shook his head. "I guess I've known all along that I was in a no-win situation. His timing did come as a surprise though. I really thought he was going to keep me around until you finally caved and did what he expected of you. Instead, he told me right after I came back after Thanksgiving that my services were no longer needed." He gave a humorless chuckle. "It was the first vacation I'd taken in years, and he fires me."

"I don't understand why he fired you. Was it because of what I said to him?"

Kenneth shrugged. "I don't know anything about that. He said it was time for you to step up, and I was holding you back."

Jeremy frowned. "How exactly did he think you were holding me back?"

"I guess I did my job too well." He gave a humorless laugh. "Or maybe I should say I did your job too well. I've been doing what he wanted you to do. Because I was good at it and enjoyed doing it, you had an excuse not to get as involved as he wanted. According to his thinking, if I'm no longer there, you will have to step up and take over."

"No one is going to take over while he is still alive," Jeremy stated. "I have tried to tell both him and Victoria that I don't want to be the CEO. I'm not cut out for that job. Neither of them believes me." He ran his long fingers through his hair.

"I'm sorry this happened, Kenneth. I never expected him to fire you."

Kenneth shrugged. "It was inevitable. I knew I was walking a narrow line. At least he gave me a good severance and a glowing recommendation."

"Glowing? That doesn't sound like something Jacob would do."

Kenneth laughed. "You're right. It was glowing coming from him. It won't be hard for me to find something else. It was time for me to move on. My girlfriend has been after me to move here anyway."

"Here? Where is here?"

"My girlfriend is from Texas," he explained. "She asked me to spend Thanksgiving with her family. Instead of just the four days, I decided to take the entire week off and flew down."

"Down where?" Jeremy got an odd feeling in his stomach.

"Her family lives in Austin." He paused, giving Jeremy a strange look. "What's wrong?" Jeremy had taken a step away from him.

"Did you come to Promise the day after Thanksgiving?" Austin was only an hour's drive from Promise.

Kenneth shook his head. "I just told you I spent the week in Austin with my girlfriend's family. Why would you think I came here?"

"Because someone shot Shep, my cousin," he clarified.

"And you think I did that?" he asked indignantly. "Why would you think I shot someone I've never met?"

"Shep and I look enough alike to be brothers," Jeremy answered. "Maybe Shep was shot by mistake."

"Boy, you're a chip off the old block after all. I thought only Jacob could be that suspicious of everyone. I guess I was wrong. You can call Amanda, my girlfriend. She'll verify I was in Austin for the entire week. That should be far enough away to give me a solid alibi." He turned to leave. He'd had enough of this family.

"Wait," Jeremy stopped him. "I'm sorry." He ran his fingers through his hair again. "That came out all wrong. I didn't mean it to sound like I was accusing you of anything."

"No?" Kenneth cocked his head to one side. "The thought must have been there, or you wouldn't have jumped to that conclusion. Why would I want to shoot you?"

"I don't know." He shook his head. "The sheriff asked if I had any enemies back home. I couldn't think of anyone but when Jacob fired you..." He shrugged.

"Jacob fired me so you jump to the conclusion that I wanted you dead. Boy, your family is really screwed up. I guess I'm glad I'm not a Fallon after all."

"Yeah, I know what you mean. Sometimes I wish I wasn't. I really am sorry for ever thinking you would do something like that." He held out his hand.

After a brief moment, Kenneth clasped his hand, accepting his apology. "Now can we discuss what I came here to tell you?"

Jeremy chuckled. "Sure. Maybe we could go inside where it isn't quite so cold."

"Cold?" Kenneth looked at him like he was out of his mind. "This is nice. You've missed some pretty bad storms back home."

Jeremy laughed. "A few short weeks ago, I said the same thing when Dan suggested it was cold here. I don't miss the cold at all."

~~~

Who is that guy? Is he another Fallon? They were multiplying like rabbits around here. I'm going to rid this town of the vermin. They all need to go down for what they did to me. I lost everything because of one person. They will lose everything because of me.

CHAPTER SIXTEEN

Jeremy's face heated up when Mona came out of the kitchen as he led Kenneth inside. "Um, Mona, this is my cousin on Victoria's side. I hope you don't mind me inviting him in."

"Now, why would I mind? Any family of yours is a family of ours." She stretched out her hand in welcome to him. "What brings you to Promise?"

"I'm visiting my girlfriend's family in Austin. Actually, she's now my fiancée," he corrected himself. "I asked her to marry me on Thanksgiving."

Jeremy had never seen his cousin this happy. Was it the fiancée or the fact that he no longer worked for Jacob? It was something to think about.

"Since I'm that close, I thought I'd drop by. I have some business matters to discuss with Jeremy."

"Oh, of course, I'll let the two of you alone. Would you like to go into the den where you can have some privacy?"

Kenneth chuckled. "There's nothing secret about what I'm going to say."

"In that case, would you like some coffee, iced tea, cookies?"

Kenneth gave a full laugh at that. "You sound like my future mother-in-law. She is always trying to feed me."

"Then I'm in good company," Mona joked. "I'll bring out some cookies."

"So, what did you want to discuss?" Jeremy led Kenneth into the great room.

"I've heard about your idea with the wind farm. I don't know why Jacob isn't interested other than he didn't think of it. I wish you had talked it over with me first."

Jeremy frowned. "How would that have changed the outcome? He still wouldn't like the idea coming from you."

"No, he wouldn't," Kenneth nodded agreement. "But we

could have figured out a way to make it seem like it was his idea instead of yours."

Jeremy nodded. He saw the advantage of that, but it was too late now. Jacob knew he wanted to start manufacturing the components for the turbines. "There's nothing I can do about that now."

"No, but I think you've got the brains to do this on your own. Don't let Jacob beat you down. If he won't help you, I will. Not financially," he quickly added with a laugh. "I'm unemployed at the moment. But I'll help you set up a business plan you can take to a bank. I'm sure you can get the financing on your own. How long are you staying here?"

"Um, I'd like to stay here as long as they'll let me. I'm not sure I'm even welcome back in Kansas City."

"You can stay here as long as you like, Jeremy." Mona came in with a tray of cookies and frosted glasses of iced tea. She smiled at them. "I'm sorry. I couldn't help but overhear the last thing you said. There's no rush for you to leave."

"You're leaving?" Bailey was only a few steps behind her mother. Tears illuminated her green eyes. "But I thought…"

"No, I'm not going anywhere." Jeremy jumped up. "That isn't what I said."

Within minutes the entire Baker household had congregated in the great room. Jeremy introduced Kenneth who seemed shell-shocked as people began asking questions and giving opinions.

"Because of Christmas and everything else that's been happening, we haven't had a chance to find out more about your idea," Dan said.

Before he could finish his thought, Kenneth gasped. "That young woman who was murdered, wasn't her body found somewhere around here? Was she a friend of your family? I didn't even think about that when I came here. I just wanted to talk to Jeremy."

Dan nodded solemnly. "Yes, we knew her. It's been a tough time for everyone in the area." Jose had been able to keep it out of the news exactly where her body was found. He hoped it remained like that. There were a lot of sick people who would want to see where she was found. They didn't want strangers wandering all over their ranch trampling things and scaring the horses and cattle.

"I came here without thinking. I'm sorry." Standing up, he turned to Jeremy. "I shouldn't have come here while you're all dealing with the murder of a friend. We can talk about this some other time. You have my cell phone number. Call me when you can." He started to hurry out.

"Wait, Kenneth." Jeremy followed him out to the porch. "You don't need to leave. Everyone is understandably upset by her death, but she wasn't a close friend. I'd like to hear what you have to say."

"Another time. I just didn't think before coming here." He stretched out his hand. "I wish you good luck, whatever you decide to do."

Jeremy stood on the porch, watching as Kenneth pulled onto the road. He had gone back inside when he heard the screech of tires and a crash. "Call 911," he called over his shoulder as he loped down the steps to his car. Had Kenneth been so upset when he left that he didn't pay attention when he went around the curve?

It took only a few minutes for him to reach the crash site. The front end of the car was smashed into a tree on the opposite side of the road. Whatever happened, the car had crossed the center line.

Kenneth's car was the only one around. Had he lost control on the curve? He hadn't been driving fast when he pulled out of the lane. The driver's side door was open. "Kenneth, where are you?" Jeremy looked around. If he'd been thrown out, he had to be close by. Jeremy stepped down into the shallow ditch, ignoring the fact he was wearing his new boots.

Dan pulled up behind Jeremy's car. The wail of sirens could be heard coming closer. "What happened? Where's

Kenneth?"

"I don't know. The car door was open when I got here, but I can't find him." He was beginning to freak out. How could he disappear in a matter of minutes?

The sheriff's SUV pulled to a stop alongside the road. "What happened?" Jeremy tried to remain calm as he explained who Kenneth was and that he'd heard the crash only minutes after he left the lane to the house. "There weren't any other vehicles here when you arrived?" Jeremy shook his head. "Then he has to be here."

There was blood on the steering wheel and blood smeared on the inside door frame where he might have put his hand when he got out of the vehicle. "It doesn't look like he was thrown out." Jose looked around. There were trees and tall grass along the road and in the ditch. "If he walked away, he couldn't have gone far in the short amount of time before you got here. Spread out and keep looking."

An hour later there was still no sign of Kenneth. "How could he just disappear?" Jeremy was in panic mode.

"Are you sure there weren't any vehicles leaving the scene when you got here?" Jose pressed. In the short distance from the ranch lane, he couldn't have gone far on his own. "Those skid marks say something happened to make him slam on the breaks."

"No." Jeremy shook his head. "If there was another vehicle here, it had to be in the middle of the road." He looked around. As far as the eye could see, the land belonged to either Dan and Mona or Ralph and Lena. The nearest neighbor was several miles in either direction. There were plenty of dirt lanes leading for the highway, but they only went onto Baker land.

"All right, I'll check with dispatch to see if anyone called in an accident, and check with the clinics and hospital. If there was another vehicle here, someone might have pulled him out and taken him to the hospital or clinic." Jose scratched his head. Was this another crime tied to Jeremy Fallon? He needed to dig a little deeper into this guy's background.

"Someone can't simply disappear," Jeremy kept repeating that. "He has to be out there somewhere. We can't give up."

"Son, we've been lookin' for the better part of five hours. If he had been injured and wandered off, he couldn't have gone far in the time it took you to get here." Dan clasped the younger man's shoulder reassuringly. "Not much to see once the sun goes down."

Shep had brought Gus out hoping to find some trace of what had happened to Kenneth. He lost the scent in the middle of the road. "Probably someone picked him up. I've checked with the hospitals and clinics. No one brought in an injured person."

"What am I supposed to tell his fiancée? I don't even know her name or how to get in touch with her?" Kenneth's phone hadn't been in the car when the sheriff searched it. Either he had it on him when he got out of the car or it got thrown out at the time of the crash. If that was the case, they would hear it ring when he called the number. There was nothing.

As much as he hated making the call to his great-grandparents, he couldn't think of any other way to find a number for this woman.

"What do you mean Kenneth is missing? Where the hell is he?" Jacob snapped before Jeremy could explain further.

"If I knew that, he wouldn't be missing." Jeremy was tired; he didn't need a hassle from Jacob.

"Women murdered, men being abducted, you need to come home immediately."

"Great-grandfather, if you say that one more time, I'm going to hang up and I will never speak to you again." Jeremy spoke through gritted teeth. There were dual gasps on the other end of the line. "If Barnard's father was as single-minded as you are about that company and everyone obeying him, I can understand why he walked away without looking back."

He drew in a deep breath, hoping to calm down some. "I didn't call to argue with you. I didn't think you'd care."

"What do you mean we wouldn't care," Victoria interrupted. "Of course we care. He is, after all, family of a sort."

"Of a sort?" Jeremy rubbed his hands over his face. This wasn't getting him anywhere. Ignoring her comment, he continued. "I only called to see if you had a telephone number for Kenneth's girlfriend, um I mean his fiancée. I need to let her know he's missing."

"His fiancée," Victoria asked. "He never told us he was getting married."

"Gee, the way you've treated him for years, I can't understand why he wouldn't tell you." Sarcasm dripped from his voice. He didn't need this. "Do you have any number I can call?"

"Since he didn't bother to tell us he was getting married, I don't know why you would think he'd give us a number for this woman," Jacob said.

Was that anger or hurt in the old man's voice? Probably anger, Jeremy decided. Jacob didn't like being in the dark about anything. He didn't know why it mattered to the older couple though. Victoria might claim Kenneth as part of her family now, but she had never acted that way toward him in all the time Kenneth had worked for the company.

"I need to go. If you could check with some of his co-workers, maybe he told them who she is."

"Are you coming home?" Jacob put it in the form of a question instead of an order.

"No. I need to help find Kenneth."

"Then you'll be home."

There's the order, Jeremy thought with a sigh. "I don't know when I'll be back." He refused to knuckle under, or even call Kansas home any longer. "I'll talk to you later." Before they could argue the point, he disconnected the call. He was grateful for all that they had done for him in his life. But gratitude only went so far. He couldn't let them run his life, or he might as well be a robot.

The next call wasn't going to be any easier, Jeremy thought. Kenneth's parents needed to be told he was missing. He probably should have called them first. Considering the way Victoria and Jacob always treated her side of the family, it was a wonder they even wanted Kenneth to work for Jacob.

Because he was a part of management at Fallon Industries, he had access to employee files. That was the only way he would be able to get the phone number for Kenneth's parents. He wasn't sure what kind of reception he would get from them since Jacob had fired their son. Hopefully, they would have the number for his fiancée.

"Why did he go to see you?" Jeremy could hear the accusation in Mrs. Stratford's voice. "Mr. Fallon fired him last week. Why would he want to see you? You're getting the job he should have. What are you doing in Texas?" Anger seemed to cancel out her worry about her son.

"I'm visiting family here. I'm not real clear on why he came to see me. I didn't know Jacob had fired him until Christmas morning I am sorry about that. It's always been my intention for Kenneth to become CEO of Fallon Industries, not me." He wasn't sure why he was explaining all of this to her. Shouldn't she be more concerned that her son was missing?

"I was hoping you could give me the phone number for…" He wasn't sure how to continue. If he hadn't told his parents he was getting married, this wasn't the way for them to find out.

"His fiancée," she finished for him. "They were here for Christmas then flew to Austin to be with Amanda's family the next day." A hint of bitterness replaced the anger in her voice.

"Do you have her number? I need to call her about what happened."

"I knew something bad had happened when he didn't call me." There were tears in Amanda's voice a few minutes later. "What happened? He was hopeful when he went to see you."

"Hopeful about what?"

"I'm not sure. He said you had some big idea he wanted to help you with. He said Mr. Fallon refused to help you with it. That man is so hateful," she wailed. "He fired Kenny after all the work he's done for that company."

"I know. I'm sorry." He didn't know what else to say. "I'll let you know when I hear anything."

"Does this have anything to do with that young woman that was killed? Did the same person do something to Ken?" She was more worried about Kenneth than his mother had been.

"The sheriff is still looking into the murder. I don't know how it could be connected to what happened to Kenneth though." Setting down the phone, he scrubbed his hands over his face. Kenneth had been missing eight hours already. He'd always heard that the first twenty-four to forty-eight hours after an abduction were the most critical. After that, the chances of finding the person alive diminish greatly.

Sheriff Garcia was waiting for him in the great room with the rest of the family. "We need to talk."

Sinking down onto the loveseat, Jeremy nodded wearily. How much more could happen?

"Since the news that Rosie Shepard and Barnard Fallon were the birth parents of Ralph Baker broke there's been a lot of vandalism 'round here," the sheriff said. "I'm not sure what that has to do with anythin', but I'm beginin' to think they have to be connected. It's gotten worse since you arrived."

Jeremy shrugged. "Okay, tell me how. I never met Kylie Turner. I met her dad for the first time a few days after she went missing."

When Bailey started to defend Jeremy, Dan put his hand on her arm, giving his head a shake. If this was all connected to the Fallons, they had to know why.

"Did you ask your great-grandparents if they knew anythin' about Bill Hancock?"

Jeremy shook his head. "Sorry, I didn't even think about

him. I don't know how they would know anything about him. My dad went to college at the University of Kansas at Kansas City. I'm not sure how much Jacob and Virginia would know about anyone he met there. My father left when I was two or three. If he met Mr. Hancock after that, I wouldn't have any way of knowing about that and neither would Jacob and Victoria."

"What did your dad do before he left?"

Jeremy shook his head. "I don't know."

"Why did he leave?"

"I'm sorry. I don't have any answers. Jacob says he left because he's weak like Barnard was. I'm not real sure what he means by that. I think it took a lot of guts to walk away from his family like that. He's also said I have too much of Barnard in me. In his eyes that isn't a compliment. I can't believe any of what's happening now has anything to do with Barnard. He's been dead for over sixty years."

Jose stood up. "Okay. Get some rest tonight. We'll start lookin' again at first light. I don't know how Kylie's murder and this are connected, but my gut tells me there is a link somewhere. It's all connected to the Fallons somehow."

"You think my coming here started all of this," Jeremy said. "Will it all stop if I leave?"

"No," Bailey whispered the word. She didn't want him to leave just when they were beginning to fall in love. This was a repeat of what happened to Rosie and Barnard. Was there someone who didn't want them to be together? That didn't make any sense.

Jose thought about Jeremy's question for a minute, then shook his head. "Whatever set this off isn't gonna go away. As long as you're here, we can catch this SOB."

"Just as long as no one else gets hurt," Jeremy said. "I don't see how any of this connects to Kylie Turner though. She's too young to have even known my dad. I doubt Turner knew him either. The only thing my dad is interested in is art, the people who create it, and the people who buy it."

"Maybe not, but it's a question I intend to ask him." Settling his big hat on his head, he headed for the door.

~~~

They're running around like chickens with their heads cut off. That makes it easier for me. They aren't gonna find this Fallon until I'm ready. They need to suffer the way I've suffered all these years first.

The lone figure turned away as the sheriff pulled out of the lane.

CHAPTER SEVENTEEN

"Why would you think I know this Davis Fallon character?" Roger Turner stood blocking the door to keep the sheriff from coming inside. "I never heard of any of them until that Jeremy guy showed up in town." That was when he did some research. The guy's great-grandparents were made of money. It still galled him that the guy walked out before he could make his sales pitch.

Why didn't people see that it would be good for the local businesses to have something like his resort in the area? Rich people would spend a lot of money in this one-horse town. Of course, he would also make a lot of money, but that was beside the point. Shouldn't the developer take the biggest share of the pot? He needed money to make money or his development was dead in the water.

The money from Kylie's insurance policy would keep the wolf from the door until he could sell more of his mini ranches. But the insurance company was stalling on paying the claim. *They have to wait for the official police report*, he thought sneeringly. Someone killed her. What more did they need to know?

The agent he'd talked to hadn't come right out and said it, but they suspected he had something to do with Kylie's murder. Maybe a quarter of a million dollars gave him a motive in their eyes, but he hadn't done this.

When he started making plans for his resort development he had increased the amount of insurance on both Kylie and his wife. The agent hadn't been opposed to it then. He got a pretty big commission from it. A lot of good it was doing him now. It made him a suspect in the eyes of the insurance company. What about the sheriff?

The sheriff was watching him closely. "Is there something else you need, Sheriff? I'm still trying to plan a funeral. The fact that I have no idea when you're going to release my daughter's body is making a difficult situation even more difficult."

"I'm sorry about that, but there are still a lot of questions surrounding her death."

"Don't you mean murder?"

"Yes, that's exactly what I mean and that's why I can't release her body just yet. Where did you go to college?"

"What?" Roger frowned at him. "What does that have to do with anything?"

"I'm just tryin' to cover all the bases. You did go to college, didn't you?"

"Yes, I went to college. What are you implying?"

"Where?" The sheriff ignored his question. He waited in silence for Turner to answer.

Roger's mind was racing. What did it matter where he'd gone to college? What did that have to do with anything? He'd been telling people he'd graduated from Texas A&M for years. He did have an honorary degree from the university. That should count for something. He wasn't sure what it would do to his business if people knew he had lied, and he didn't want to find out.

The silence stretched out for several long moments, becoming oppressive. "I went to a small community college," he finally blurted out.

"Where?" Jose asked again.

Turner heaved a sigh. "Dallas. What does that have to do with anything?"

"Like I said, just covering all the bases. You ever been to Kansas City?"

"Is this a fishing expedition of some kind?" The sheriff lifted his shoulders, one corner of his mouth quirking upward slightly. "If you have any more questions, feel free to contact my lawyer." He slammed the door shut. The lock clicked loudly into place.

The sheriff chuckled. He did love yankin' the chain of folks he thought were a little on the shady side. He wasn't sure whether Turner had anything to do with his daughter's death or the disappearance of Kenneth Stratford. But there was one thing he was fairly certain of: the man wasn't on the up and up. If he was living on borrowed money and running out of time, would he be desperate enough to kill his only child for the insurance money?

The insurance agent had contacted him shortly after her body had been found. A quarter of a million dollars would certainly ease Turner's money troubles. He hadn't generated enough interest in his development to sell off what he had already built.

It would be nice to get a look at his finances. So far, he didn't have just cause to bring before a judge to get a warrant. Until that happened, he needed to concentrate on finding Kenneth Stratford.

~~~

"Hello? Is anyone there? Where am I? Please talk to me. Tell me what's going on. Why are you doing this?" He could hear faint scratching noises, but no one answered him. Were there rats in this…? Was he in a building of some sort? He had no idea where he was. Rats carry all kinds of diseases. He didn't want to get bit. Wild animals could do a lot more damage. But the biggest threat was the person who was doing this.

He was blindfolded, his arms were tied behind his back, and his ankles were tied together. He could feel dirt and grit on the floor beneath him and something solid behind his back. How long had he been here?

Trying to recall what had happened caused his head to hurt. After he'd been to see Jeremy, he was heading back to Austin. The road curved and… Nothing. His mind was blank until he woke up here, wherever here is.

At a scraping sound somewhere in the room, he scooted his back up against the wall. Heavy footsteps came close to him. "Who's there? Why are you doing this?"

"I have water for you. Shut up and drink." The voice was

harsh and muffled so he couldn't tell if this was a man or a woman. The lip of a plastic bottle was pressed against his mouth.

Until the cool liquid filled his mouth, he hadn't realized how thirsty he was. That had to mean he'd been there for a long while. Mrs. Baker had invited him to stay for lunch before he left the ranch, but he'd declined. Now he wished he'd stayed. Breakfast was the only thing he'd had to eat since nine that morning when he left Austin. Thinking of food, his stomach growled.

It had been noon when he left the Baker ranch. By now people had to know he was missing. Would they be able to find him before he either died of thirst, hunger, or a wild animal killed him? The two-legged animals were the most deadly and the ones he feared the most.

When the bottle was empty, the person replaced it with something hard and crunchy. "Eat." The same voice growled at him.

Okay, this person was going to keep him alive, but for how long? Why had he been abducted? *Ransom*, the thought struck him like a fist to the gut. "I'm not rich," he spoke around the crunchy bar the person was shoving in his mouth. "My family can't pay any ransom."

"Shut up or I'll stop feedin' you."

Kenneth tried to detect a speech pattern or something he would be able to identify later. The only thing he could say was the person had a Texas drawl. No help there, he decided since he was in Texas.

Swallowing the last bite of the crunchy bar, he was still hungry. "Can I have more?"

"That's enough. I'm not tryin' to fatten you up like a head of cattle," was the harsh reply.

By now Kenneth assumed he was dealing with a man, but the voice was too gravelly to be certain. He didn't know if the person was trying to disguise his voice or if he'd smoked too many cigarettes over his lifetime.

"Why are you doing this to me? What did I do to you?"

"The Fallons have to pay for what they've done."

"My name isn't Fallon." For that, he received a sharp slap across his face.

"I know who you are. I saw you. Don't try denyin' it. You're all gonna pay." Heavy footsteps marched to what he assumed was a door that scrapped open. It slammed shut hard enough to make the wall he was leaning against wobble.

If this was about Jacob Fallon, there could be any number of people that wanted the man to pay for something he'd done to them. The man was ruthless when it came to business. Anything else, he simply ignored. How could he convince this person he wasn't a Fallon?

Fallon Industries did business with other companies all over the country and some outside of the country. That meant there could be a lot of enemies wanting to get even with Jacob. But why had he been the chosen scapegoat? He didn't even work for the man any longer. If this person tried to get Jacob to pay ransom to save Kenneth, he was toast. Jacob wouldn't lift a finger to save him.

~~~

Jeremy wasn't a very good horseman, but he insisted on helping in the search for Kenneth. If the sheriff was right, he was the catalyst behind Kylie's murder and Kenneth's abduction. He couldn't sit around doing nothing.

They had searched areas close to where Kenneth's car had gone off the road the day before. They were going to expand the search now. The only way he could have gotten so far from the crash site was with someone moving him.

As far as the eye could see, the land belonged to Don or Ralph Baker. The first place Jose wanted to check out was the shack on Ralph Baker's ranch where Kylie's body had been found. If someone was using that as a dump spot, he wanted to know about it.

There were woods, streams, marshland, and just about anything in between all across the area. That meant there were plenty of places to dispose of a body. Jose didn't know why someone was doing this, but he intended to find out. He didn't like someone messing with the people he was charged with protecting.

Ralph's ranch butts up to Dan's on one side and what used to be Weston's ranch on the other side. That was the part that Weston had sold off to Turner. It was one more reason the Bakers hadn't been happy with Turner's development. There was still a lot of open range between Ralph's house and the mini-mansions Turner was building, but Baker still wasn't happy about the land being developed. It had been open range for hundreds of years. That's the way it should stay.

Ranchers and folks from town had joined in to help with the search even though they didn't know Kenneth. Elliott Weston was one of those helping, but not by choice. "I don't know why you had to drag me out here," he grumbled to Sue Ann. "I never met the guy."

"Someone is doin' this to our neighbors," Sue Ann said. She was disgusted with her lazy husband.

"That guy ain't no neighbor," Elliott continued to complain. "He don't live here. I don't even know his name."

"He's that young Fallon guy's cousin or somethin' of the sort."

"He ain't no neighbor either. He'll be goin' back where he belongs real soon."

Sue Ann glared at her husband. She wished she'd never married the lazy SOB. The only good thing that came out of her marriage to Elliott Weston was her son. Looking at Sam, her soft smile made her plain face almost pretty. Sam and the ranch, she amended. But half of that was gone now. For a measly pile of money, he sold off his family's land. What was he gonna leave his only son now?

She spurred her horse forward, leaving her husband to fend for himself. Like any other day, she and Sam would be pulling Elliott's weight as well as their own. Maybe she should have left him home like he wanted. Listening to him complain all day was gonna make a long day seem even longer. Looking back over her life there were only a few high points. Elliott Weston wasn't one of them.

"Don't know why we'd need to search this place." They rode up to the edge of what used to be Weston land. "There's no place here to dump a body."

"How would you know?" Sue Ann glared at him. "You haven't checked out here long before you sold out to Turner."

Elliott shrugged one shoulder like he was too lazy to lift both of them. "Turner's building our future out here."

"Our future, my eye. Far as I can tell, the guy's all blow and no show." She nudged her horse forward. It was long before Elliott sold off the land when she last explored the back acres. There were even a few old bunkhouses that Elliott's great-grandfather built when he first started ranching.

Elliott pulled a bottle of whiskey out of his saddlebag. If he had to be out here, he might as well enjoy himself. "Put that away," Sue Ann ordered when she looked over her shoulder at him. "This isn't supposed to be a party. If Jose sees you drinkin' he's not gonna be happy."

"He ain't nowhere 'round." His words were already beginning to slur. How much had he been drinking when she didn't notice? "It's hot out here. A guy needs to stay hyd… um hyp…" Unable to find the right word, he shrugged. "Gotta drink a lot of liquor when it's hot."

"It's not that hot. And it's liquid, not liquor you're supposed to drink, you fool," she said in disgust. "Alcohol isn't gonna help you stay hydrated." She turned her horse away again. Maybe he'll get drunk enough to fall into the creek and drown. Could she be so lucky?

They hadn't gone far when a Polaris four-wheeler roared over a small rise. "What the hell do you think you're doing on my land?" Vandals had set a fire in the living room of one of the houses he was building, and he'd been checking it out when he saw the horses.

Sue Ann's horse reared nearly unseating her when the big

machine stopped in front of him. The horse was skittish enough. She didn't need something like this scaring him.

"We're out searchin' for that missing dude," Elliott said. "Not doing no harm."

So that's why the sheriff had been at his place earlier. "Well, there isn't anyone here, so you can take yourselves off my land. I have construction workers coming today." That was a lie, but they didn't need to know that.

"Used to be my land," Elliott said. "This here project you got going has my name on it, too."

Turner gritted his teeth. That had been his second mistake. Weston wanted top dollar for the land, and he wanted it in cash. When he couldn't come up with the full asking price, he agreed the guy could be a partner in the deal. So far, he hadn't done anything to bring in business.

"What makes you think the guy is anywhere near this place. My daughter was found on Baker's land. Maybe he did something to this guy, too."

"You thinkin' old man Baker killed your daughter?" Sue Ann looked down on Turner from her high perch on the horse. "Why would he do somethin' like that? The Bakers are all upstandin' folks."

"Right, and I'm not?" He glared at her. "If you want to search my property, get a search warrant." He snapped his fingers. "Oh, that's right, you don't have probable cause." He chuckled.

"You're makin' yourself look guilty," Sue Ann said.

Turning the big Polaris around, he looked over his shoulder at her. "Prove it."

CHAPTER EIGHTEEN

Three days later Kenneth was still missing. For the second time in less than a month, Jose stood before the cameras asking for help finding another young person who had gone missing in his jurisdiction. This didn't look good for his county but that was the least of his worries.

If Kenneth had simply wandered off after the accident, he would have been found by that time. There were no mountain cliffs for him to fall off, but there were plenty of streams and rivers he could drown in.

Even that scenario came up short. Those streams and rivers were miles away from where Kenneth's car had crashed into the tree. He couldn't have gotten that far on his own without leaving some sort of trail.

In the hope that Gus would be able to follow a scent, Shep had brought the dog with them. Again they came up empty. Whoever was behind this had managed to leave no scent trail for Gus to follow.

Did that mean his kidnapper knew about Gus? Shep wondered. That would mean his abductor knew the family. Why would anyone in Promise kidnap Kenneth? He'd only been in town a few hours when this happened. Jeremy was the only person he knew in Promise.

By now, everyone assumed Kenneth had been kidnapped, but without a ransom demand, no one knew why he had been taken. The longer the search went on the more it looked like it would be a recovery instead of a rescue.

There didn't seem to be any connection between Jeremy and what was happening. Yet there was no other explanation. Jacob Fallon wanted Jeremy to return to Kansas and accept his place in the family company. Until now Kenneth had been the one Jeremy kept insisting should take over.

How would Kenneth being kidnapped entice Jeremy to return to Kansas and follow in his great-grandfather's footsteps? Even that didn't make sense. Jacob had fired Kenneth before this happened. He had no reason to have Kenneth kidnapped.

Where did Kylie's murder fit in? Again, nothing was making sense.

The road where the crash occurred traveled through the Baker ranch. It stood to reason the search would be headquartered at the Lazy B. The women had kept coffee and sandwiches ready for the searchers as they returned to base. At the end of the day, the weary group had just returned when a big Town Car pulled into the lane.

"Great-grandmother?" Jeremy stared at the older woman when she stepped out of the car. His great-grandfather opened the driver's side door. "What are you doing here?" He stared at them. "How did you get here?"

"We flew here of course," Jacob said as Jeremy walked over to them. His faded eyes traveled over his great-grandson, taking in his dusty clothes and weary expression. "What have you been doing?" A frown drew his bushy eyebrows together.

"I've been helping to search for Kenneth. What are you doing here?" he asked again.

"Well, you followed us to Iowa last summer to see what we were up to. I thought we should return the favor and see what you were up to." Was he joking? Jeremy couldn't be sure. He'd never known the man to have a sense of humor.

"Hello," Mona came up behind Jeremy. "I'm Mona Baker. Welcome to the Lazy B." She reached out to shake their hands.

Victoria hesitantly accepted her handshake, while Jacob ignored her altogether. Jeremy's face turned pink at the slight. If they weren't even going to be civil, why had they come?

"Have you found Kenneth?" Victoria asked. Was that concern he heard in her voice? "His mother is worried and blames us for anything that happens to her son."

Ah, the truth comes out. She didn't really care about Kenneth; she just didn't want to be blamed for whatever happened to him. "No, we haven't found him." He couldn't keep the chill out of his voice. These people weren't even nice. How had he missed that fact all these years?

"Shall we go inside?" Mona offered. "Everyone is tired after a long day searching. Can I get you some coffee, or something stronger? I'm sure you're both worried about your nephew."

"He's my wife's great-nephew," Jacob qualified. To him, there was a big difference. Even in a situation like this, he wouldn't claim him as a relative.

"Coffee would be nice." Victoria accepted Mona's offer. "What they offered on the flight here could barely be called coffee."

Jeremy's face turned pink at the pompous tone in Victoria's voice. These were the people who raised him. He said a prayer that he wouldn't turn out like them in his old age. But this is the way they have always been, he reminded himself. They always thought they were better than the average person.

Jeremy was torn whether to help the others with the horses or go inside with Jacob and Victoria. Leaving them alone with Mona, there was no telling how rude they would be. "The guys will take care of the horses," Bailey whispered as she came up beside him. It was like she knew he needed her moral support where his great-grandparents were concerned.

"What have you learned about Kenneth?" Jacob got right to the point once they were seated in the great room.

"We're still searching," Jeremy said. "We don't know where he is." He walked across the room to sit next to Bailey.

"Jeremy, you're all dirty," Victoria admonished him. "You need to wash up."

His face flamed hot. How could she treat him like he was three years old in front of Bailey and Mona? "I'll wash later." He spoke through gritted teeth. "I'm assuming you came here to find out about Kenneth, not teach me about hygiene."

Bailey sat down next to him, taking his hand in hers. She

was every bit as dirty as Jeremy since she had joined in the search. Her heart went out to him. It was understandable that he wanted to get away from his great-grandparents if this was how they always treated him.

He smiled at her simple gesture of support. It meant the world to him when Victoria had attempted to humiliate him. He knew in his heart that he was in love with this gentle, fierce, feisty, loyal woman. She would always stand behind and beside him.

Before the conversation deteriorated further, Dan and the others came in from the kitchen. They had left their dirty boots at the back door and shook as much of the dust off their clothes as possible. They looked bone-weary after three days of unsuccessful searching.

Parker's mom had diverted her husband and the twins before going into the great room. Jeremy didn't need an audience. He needed to face his great-grandparents. If there were others around, he might hold back when he shouldn't.

She caught Jeremy's eye before she ushered them up the back stairs. With a grateful nod in her direction, he introduced the rest of Shep's family. He watched Jacob making sure he didn't insult these people. If that happened, he was ready to tell them both to leave. That sort of behavior might be acceptable with their friends in Kansas, but he wouldn't put up with it now. Maybe that was why they didn't have many friends.

Dan looked at his grubby hands and brushed them against the leg of his jeans. "You'll have to forgive me for not offerin' to shake hands. We've been on horseback since daylight searchin' for your nephew."

"He's my wife's great-nephew," Jacob corrected, with a pompous attitude. "We came to see what's being done to find him. I had no idea he would come here to see Jeremy after he left the company."

"Call a spade a spade, Great-grandfather," Jeremy said. "You fired him." His tone was harsh.

"I thought it was time for him to find his own place in the world. He was becoming too comfortable in his position."

"You thought you could force me to take a job I didn't want and wouldn't be good at if Kenneth wasn't there," Jeremy argued.

Jacob didn't bother to disagree with that point. He knew Jeremy was right. "I never meant for anything bad to happen to him. I thought it was best for all concerned."

"You thought it was the best way to get what you wanted." Jeremy stood up hoping they would take the hint and leave. "I'm sorry, Great-grandfather. I'm too tired for this tonight. Once we've found Kenneth, we can discuss this, but you need to know I'm not going to change my mind. I am not going to take over running Fallon Industries."

He left them little choice but to leave. Mona graciously invited them for dinner, but to Jeremy's relief, they declined. He released the breath he was holding once their car was out of sight. What was he going to do if they stayed until Kenneth was found? What did they think that would accomplish? Running his long fingers through his hair, he realized how dusty he really was. With a small laugh, he shook his head. Victoria must have been appalled at his appearance. He didn't even care.

Back inside, he turned to the others. "I need to apologize for the way my great-grandparents acted. I never expected them to show up here."

"You don't need to apologize for anything," Dan said. "What they do and how they act is on them." Someone's stomach rumbled with hunger then, and he laughed. "I think we all need to wash up and get some grub. That sandwich was good, but it is nothin' but a distant memory now."

~~~

News travels fast in a small town. That bastard Jacob Fallon is now on my turf. I couldn't compete before. Let's see how he likes playing by my rules this time. He's gonna pay for everything he and that bastard grandson of his did to me.

"Once we've located Kenneth, Shep and I would like to hear more about your idea of a wind farm and individual wind turbines for houses," Parker told Jeremy later that evening. "I'm not sure if you know that we've helped out several people. We'd like to do the same for you."

Jeremy stared at them, unsure what to say. First Kenneth wanted to help him get a business plan together and now Parker and Shep were willing to consider helping him. The people who were supposed to love him the most weren't willing to even listen to his idea.

"Thank you. I appreciate that. I'm not sure what Jacob and Victoria showing up here means, but it can't be good. Jacob is a force to be dealt with. He doesn't like opposition."

"We aren't opposing him." She gave a little laugh. "We're going around him. Tomorrow's another day. Let's pray that Kenneth is safe wherever he is and we find him soon." She knew the odds of that were growing slimmer and slimmer every day.

~~~

"This has been another wasted trip, just like the one last summer." Victoria glared at her husband. "If we had stayed home, Jeremy never would have known about these people. None of this would have happened."

"So you're saying this is my fault."

"That's exactly what I'm saying. These people have no interest in Fallon Industries, not to mention any legal right to the company."

"Did you see how they live?" Jacob scoffed. "The house is fairly big, but it certainly doesn't compare with what I've provided for you all these years. Are you willing to take the chance that they wouldn't jump at the opportunity to have what Fallon Industries is worth?"

She thought about that for a minute. Was it greedy that she didn't want to give up what she had to a bunch of strangers? She was too old to change now.

For long periods, Kenneth was alone in what he assumed was a lean-to or shack. Wind whistled through the boards of what remained of any walls. He had no idea where he was or why he had been kidnapped. The person came twice a day, or what he assumed was a day, to give him a bottle of water and a granola bar. Each time, his hands were untied long enough for him to relieve himself in a corner.

He could tell passage of time by the drop in temperature at night and the rise again once the sun came up. Unless he'd lost count, he'd been missing five days. Would they even continue to search for him?

If the point of all of this was to get money from Jacob, his kidnapper was going to be disappointed. Jacob wouldn't lift a finger to help him before he'd been fired. Now that he no longer worked at Fallon Industries, Jacob wouldn't care what happened to him. His one hope was Jeremy.

What would his kidnapper do if Jacob wouldn't pay the ransom? His folks were comfortably set, but they couldn't come up with several hundred thousand dollars at the drop of a hat. He knew they would do anything to save him, but they couldn't compete with the funds that were available to Jacob. He prayed that God would lead someone to where he was being kept.

CHAPTER NINETEEN

Someone knocking on their hotel room door caused Victoria to hope it might be Jeremy come to apologize for the way he nearly threw them out the night before. She was doomed to be disappointed. A gasp tore from her throat at the sight of the tall man in a sheriff's uniform standing in the hall. She wasn't as callous as her husband. She did care about Kenneth.

"D...did you find Kenneth?" The words were barely above a whisper.

"No, Ma'am. I'm sorry; I didn't mean to frighten you. I'm Sheriff Jose Garcia. I would like to have a few words with you and your husband."

"What's this about?" Jacob came up behind Victoria. They didn't bother inviting him into their room.

"I would like to ask you a few questions about your grandson."

"Jeremy is our great-grandson," the older man said, his tone haughty.

"No, Sir, I'm not talking about Jeremy. I'd like to talk to you about Davis Fallon, your grandson."

"I know who he is," Jacob snapped. "What does he have to do with Kenneth? We haven't seen Davis in several years."

"Yes, that's what Jeremy said. Did you ever know any of his friends while he was in college? Is it all right if I come in?" Victoria swayed slightly, and her face had lost color. "Are you all right, Ma'am?"

"She's worried about her great-nephew." A look that Jose couldn't interpret passed between the older couple. With a sigh that said he really didn't want to invite him into the room, Jacob took several steps aside leaving enough room for the sheriff to squeeze past. Once the door was shut, he faced the younger man. "What does Davis have to do with Kenneth being kidnapped?"

"Did you ever hear Davis talk about a man by the name of William or Bill Hancock?"

Victoria released the breath she'd been holding. This wasn't what either of them had expected the sheriff to ask.

"I don't believe I ever heard him mention anyone by that name. It's been a long time since Davis was in college. Why are you asking about that now? Who is this person?"

"He seemed to recognize the Fallon name when Jeremy first came here. He implied that he knew Davis at some point in the past."

When Jacob looked at Victoria, she gave a small shake of her head. Jacob turned back to the sheriff. "We've never heard of this person. I'm sure you have more important things to think about than a guessing game from the past." He walked over to the door, pulling it open. There was little doubt he wanted Jose to leave.

They were hiding something, Jose was sure of it. Whether it had anything to do with young Stratford's kidnapping or Bill Hancock was anyone's guess. They were a couple of cold, calculating people. He felt sorry for Jeremy. Being raised by them couldn't have been easy.

His next stop was Roger Turner's house. The man had refused to allow them to search his land without a search warrant even though it made him look guilty. His response was always "Prove it."

Elliott Weston told him there were several old bunkhouses at the back of the property. Sue Ann scoffed at that. "They should have been torn down long before Sam was born," she said. "Nobody's gone out there to check to see if they're even standing in probably fifteen years."

"You have a search warrant this time, Sheriff?" Roger Turner stepped onto the veranda when Jose got out of his SUV.

"No, I wanted to appeal to your better nature." It galled him to beg the guy to do the decent thing, but he still didn't have enough probable cause to get a search warrant.

Turner gave a bitter laugh. "I don't have a better nature since someone murdered my daughter. When you find that person, I might reconsider and let you look for this guy on my land. Until then, get off my property." He stepped back inside, slamming the door.

Jose turned away. He really hadn't expected anything different but had been hoping. He couldn't say he blamed Turner for being bitter. His only child's murderer was still enjoying life somewhere. There was no evidence at the site where her body had been found. The ME did say she had been killed somewhere else and moved to the shack later.

Bill Hancock hadn't been seen since the day he confronted Jeremy when he first came to town. But he thought that was voluntary instead of forced. He rubbed his hands over his face. He was tired, but so were a lot of other folks. His gut told him this was all focused around Jeremy Fallon, but he couldn't figure out why. The kid was squeaky clean. He'd never been in trouble. With the great-grandparents he'd been graced with, he was probably too afraid to step out of bounds.

~~~

It had been almost a month since anyone had seen Bill Hancock and he suddenly appears out of nowhere. Jose stepped out of his office. "Hey, Hancock. I've been looking for you. Where've you been?" The slightly built man stopped when the sheriff called out to him.

"I went to visit my brother. What's it to you?" It looked like his troubles were here waiting for him to come back.

"As I said, I've been looking for you. You left town pretty sudden. Mind telling me why?"

"I just needed some fresh scenery. There was a bad smell around here. I haven't done nothin' wrong. Why're you pickin' on me?" he whined.

"I'm not pickin' on you. Where's your brother live?"

"Why?" He got a bad feeling in his stomach."

"Just need to know." He waited to see what the other man would do.

"Joe lives in a little town up in the panhandle. He's got himself a hardware store. I went to help him out a little. What's this about?"

"When did you leave Promise?"

Hancock began to get jittery. This didn't look good. "I haven't done nothin' wrong," he repeated. "What's this about?"

"I need to know when you left town."

Hancock's shoulders slumped. "The day before Thanksgiving. I just got back in town. You gonna tell me why you're askin'?"

"Can anyone up there confirm your alibi?"

"Alibi?" His voice squeaked. "I don't need an alibi 'cuz I ain't done anything."

"I'm not sayin' you did. I just need to confirm where you've been for the past month."

"I was at my brother's house. I helped him out some at his store. Lots of folks saw me. They'll tell you I was there." His hands were shaking. This had to have something to do with that Fallon character. He probably told the sheriff I called his old man names. Someday he'd learn to keep his mouth shut.

"Okay," the sheriff nodded his head. "Give me his number. I'll give him a call. Don't go anywhere for the next few days."

"You tellin' me not to leave town?"

Jose laughed. "Yeah, I guess I am. See you around." He turned and headed back to his office. Hopefully, he'd finally get some answers. But if Hancock had been with his brother all this time, where did that leave his investigation?

Kenneth Stratford was still missing along with Kylie Turner's killer. Had the same person that killed Kylie kidnapped Stratford? He hadn't found a motive for either crime. Were the two connected somehow? Grabbing the keys to his SUV, he headed back to the shack where Kylie's body had been found. If he searched it often enough, he might find something he'd missed.

The players are all in place. I'm finally going to get the revenge I've waited for. It's time for this game to end.

Parker paced the length of the porch. Sitting down on the porch swing, she bounced back up. She was too agitated to sit still. Something told her things were coming to a head. People had given up finding Kenneth alive and the number of searchers was dropping daily. If he was dead, where was his body? Who would kill him?

He'd never been in Promise until the day he came to visit Jeremy. Was his disappearance connected to the murder of that young woman? Her thoughts were going in circles. Nothing added up.

Picking up on her tension, Gus paced beside her. Now and then he would stop to stare out at the field. She didn't know if he saw or heard something she couldn't see or hear. Was he trying to tell her something? Gus was good, but would he be able to sense that something was wrong with Shep? She shook her head, her red curls bouncing around her face. She was letting worry get the best of her.

Mona had joined the others in the search. Even her dad and brothers had gone with them. That left her with her mom and Lena to make sandwiches for the searchers as they came in for a break.

Laura joined her on the porch, a look of worry creasing her forehead. "There's nothing you can do out here, Honey. You need to try and relax."

"How could something like this happen, Mom? Maybe I should be used to people dying, but I'm not. My heart aches for Mr. Turner. I'm not sure he's a nice man, but his daughter didn't deserve to die because of that." In the three years she'd been in Whitehaven there had been several murders. She had even found the body of one of the victims. That didn't make this any easier.

"No, she didn't. I'm sure the sheriff will figure this out."

"Do you think Kenneth is still alive? It's possible, isn't it?" She paused for a minute. "If Uncle Abner were here he'd say it was my fault." She gave a humorless chuckle. "He has gotten better recently. His grumbles seem to be more habit now than real animosity." Abner was her grandpa's brother. He hadn't liked the fact that Rosie had left the family farm to Parker instead of him.

Laura shook her head. "Abner was the worst of all my uncles. I don't recall him ever liking anyone."

Gus gave a sharp bark, staring off into the distance. "I know, boy. You want to be out there searching along with the others." Shep wouldn't hear of it though. Gus's job was to protect Parker. That was the reason she got him when she first moved to Whitehaven. As though he understood what she said, he whined.

Parker laughed at him, roughing up his ears. "Come on, boy. Let's go for a run."

"Are you sure about that?" Laura frowned at her daughter.

"I'll be fine. The doctor said as long as I take it easy I can continue with my normal routine. Gus won't let anyone get close enough to hurt me. We'll stick to the local obstacle course. Otherwise known as the pasture," she said with a laugh. "The obstacles can get pretty squishy and smelly if I'm not careful."

For several moments, Laura watched Parker and Gus. She might not like it, but her daughter was a grown woman. She knew her limitations. She wouldn't do anything to harm the baby she was carrying. "God, protect this family," she whispered a prayer. "You know all that is going on. Please, stop the evil from hurting anyone else. Bring Kenneth back safely." Placing the family in God's hands was the best thing she could do.

In the time they'd been in Texas, Parker had gotten used to running through the pasture. It was like running around the field only here she had to watch for cow patties and horse droppings, along with gopher holes. Gus's heart wasn't in it though. This wasn't what he wanted. He wanted to be out with Shep and the others. Distracted, he kept stopping to sniff at the air. Was he able to smell danger? Is that what he was trying to tell her, that Shep was in danger?

"Okay, boy, let's go back to the porch." Neither of them felt like running. Sinking onto the swing again, she wished Gus could tell her why he was so agitated. Each time he barked at some unknown object, her stomach churned. Was someone watching them? It wouldn't be the first time someone had spied on her.

She looked around for any danger Gus might see. There was nothing but cattle and horses as far as the eye could see. Did he know more than she did? He had been out with Shep right after Kenneth's accident. He hadn't been able to detect where Kenneth had been taken. Why would he be able to lead them to where Kenneth was now? Or did he sense that Shep was in danger?

Gus stood up, peering off in the direction the men had gone just hours ago. With his snout in the air and his ears laid back, the ruff down his back stood on end. "What is it, Gus? What do you see?" Without warning, he shot off the porch. "Gus, stop." For the first time, he ignored her order. "Mom, Grams," she shouted, pulling open the door to the house. "Something happened."

The other women stepped out onto the porch. "What happened? Are you all right?"

"Gus just took off," she explained. "I think he knows Shep is in trouble."

"How could he know that?" Lena asked. "I know he's a smart dog, but knowing Shep is in trouble when he isn't even here goes beyond smart."

"I don't know." Parker pulled her cell phone out of the pocket of her jacket calling Shep. The call went straight to voice mail. "Please call me as soon as you get this. Let me know you're all right." She didn't try to explain Gus's actions because she couldn't. While she was calling Shep, Mona tried to reach Dan, and Lena tried Ralph's cell as well. They both went to voice mail.

"Something happened to them. I know it." Parker's voice was clogged with tears. "Do you know where they were searching today?" Both women shook their heads.

"Maybe they're out of cell range," Lena suggested. She prayed that was the case.

"Were Dad and the twins working in the same area as Shep?" She had her fingers crossed that they were with the sheriff. They couldn't all be out of reach.

When Ben answered his phone after three rings, Laura released the breath she'd been holding. "Where are you? Are the boys with you? Do you know where Shep and the others are?" Her questions tumbled out without giving him a chance to answer.

"Sheriff Garcia wanted to have another look at the shack where Kylie was found. He asked if I'd go along. Maybe a fresh pair of eyes would see something the others had missed. What's wrong? Is Parker okay?" There was a hint of worry in his voice. Parker's dad was a psychologist. Sometimes he could see behavior patterns that others missed.

Laura tried to explain Gus's strange behavior. "Do you know where the others are searching? Where are the boys?"

"The boys are here with the sheriff and me. Shep took Jeremy, Dan, and Ralph with him. I think they were going to stop by the Weston ranch to see if Sam and his dad would join them." He drew in a deep breath before releasing it slowly. He hesitated to put his thoughts into words. "Everyone is thinking time is running out for Kenneth," he finished on a sad note.

"They aren't answering their phones," Laura told him. "Something is wrong. The sheriff needs to find them." They had all forgotten Gus was on the job.

CHAPTER TWENTY

"The... the sheriff sent me to tell you they found your nephew." Sue Ann stammered. She had gone to the hotel where Jacob and Victoria were staying.

"He's her great-nephew." Jacob automatically corrected the woman. He had no idea who she was. If the sheriff had news about Kenneth, he should have come himself.

"Is he all right?" Victoria stepped around her husband. She had spent years caring for only two people besides herself. It was hard to change that habit. But she still didn't wish harm to come to Kenneth.

"No, I'm afraid he's in pretty bad shape." Sue Ann kept her head down, her eyes trained on the floor. "I'm sorry. I don't know if he's gonna make it."

"So what are you doing here?"

"Well, the sheriff thought you might like to see him before..." She gulped unable to finish her sentence.

"Yes, of course," Victoria said. She wasn't sure what she was supposed to feel at a time like this. She had closed off her heart to everyone but Jeremy years ago.

"Good, I'll take you to where he is." She turned away expecting the old couple to follow her.

"I thought we were going to the hospital," Jacob said as Sue Ann drove out of town.

"No, it was too dangerous to move him. I'm taking you to where he was found." The couple was sitting in the back seat of her big truck like she was their chauffeur. *It was probably the first time either of them had been in a truck*, she thought disparagingly. Even though it was top of the line, it couldn't compete with the comfort of a limo. She didn't care. Silence filled the truck after that.

"What is this place?" Jacob frowned when Sue Ann pulled up to a shack that was ready to fall down.

"It's where your nephew has been for the past week." She

opened the door for them, waiting for them to get out. Instead, they sat there like they were afraid the dirty shack would contaminate them.

"How many times do I have to tell you people that he's my wife's great-nephew, not mine? Are you too stupid to remember something as simple as that?" Could anyone be more simple-minded?

"It's not gonna matter much longer. Come on and climb on out." She'd had her fill of their pompous attitude. She was through messing with them. Taking the old lady by the arm, she hauled her out.

"Take it easy. You're hurting my wife." Jacob saw the pain on Victoria's face. "Where is the sheriff?"

"He'll be along later." She reached out to tug on his arm. He was taking too long to get out. She was in a hurry to get this done. She gave him a little shove in the back to get him walking. "Much later." She chuckled.

Pushing open the door to the small shack, Victoria gasped when she saw the men tied up alongside Kenneth. There was also a man on the dirt floor with blood seeping out of a wound in his chest. Each man was bound hand and foot. There was Duct tape over their mouths. Fear mingled with anger in the eyes of the Baker men. The fact that they weren't blindfolded left little doubt that this woman didn't care that they saw her face.

"What is this?" Jacob started to turn to glare down at the much shorter woman. "Release my great-grandson immediately." He took a step toward Jeremy. There was a lump on the side of his head that looked like a baseball had somehow lodged itself under his skin.

He received a similar lump for his effort when she hit him on the side of his head with a very lethal-looking gun. His knees buckled beneath him, and he fell at Jeremy's feet. Jeremy tried to wiggle free to reach him, but the ropes on his wrists were too tight for him to do anything.

After being blindfolded for so long, Kenneth continued to

blink his eyes at the sun shining through the warped boards in the wall and the door. He hadn't realized his capture was a woman until she had brought Jeremy and the others into the shack. He had no idea who she was, or why she had kidnapped him and the others.

He tried to move against the rope binding him to help them, but he was weak from lack of food and water. In the time he'd been held captive, the only thing he'd had to eat was two granola bars each day along with two bottles of water.

"Jeremy, Kenneth, are you boys all right?" Victoria asked. She felt a twinge of remorse for all the years she had ignored the fact Kenneth was her great-nephew. She stepped toward them.

"Stay where you are, old woman," Sue Ann snapped, glaring at the older couple. "You don't remember me, do you." It was a statement, not a question. "It doesn't matter. You'll remember by the time I'm finished here."

"Of course I don't remember you. I've never seen you before. Tell me what this is about." Used to giving orders, Jacob expected her to reply immediately.

Sue Ann gave a nasty chuckle. "You just don't get it. You aren't the one giving the orders now." She paced across the dirt floor, pointing the gun at each of them in turn. "You Fallons ruined my life," she spit the words out at Jacob. "You all think you're so much better than the rest of the world. Now, you're gonna find out what it's like to have everything taken away from you."

With wild eyes, she looked at Jeremy. "Did you know I was in love with your father at one time?" She didn't bother to wait for him to answer. "I wanted to marry him. I was going to have his baby." A sob caught in her throat. "Instead, I got stuck with this lazy son-of-a..." She pointed the gun at the man bleeding on the floor. "If things had turned out the way I wanted, you would be my son."

Shep groaned. This was a repeat of what happened to Rosie and Barnard then again to Parker's mom. Was Sue Ann as crazy as Ed Bodeen had been? Reality had loosely slipped in his mind, one minute he thought Parker was his daughter, and the next he was going to kill her because Rosie had left the house he thought should be his to Parker.

"Your great-grandfather thought his precious grandson was too good for the likes of me. He insisted your dad had to marry that hussy instead," Sue Ann continued. "You see how that turned out. We could have been happy. All she was after was his money. I would have done anything for him, gone anywhere with him. I guess his choice of a bride didn't turn out so well after all." Her laugh was slightly hysterical.

For a minute, her eyes lost focus while her mind traveled into the past. Giving herself a shake, she looked back at Jeremy. "Your bastard father made me kill my baby. I'm gonna return the favor." She raised the gun, aiming it at Jeremy. A gasp slipped past the gag covering his mouth.

"My grandson did no such thing," Jacob spoke up. His heart was in his throat. Jeremy was the most precious thing he had, other than the company he had fought for all these years. He couldn't let her kill him. The woman was delusional. He had to keep her talking. Surely, someone would rescue them. "He would never sanction killing someone."

"You sound so self-righteous with your nose in the air like I was a wet cow patty you stepped in," she sneered at him. "You threatened to have me arrested. You said I was two years older than him and I had forced him to have sex with me. It was a lie! He would have loved me and our baby." She was shouting, pointing the gun at him now. Jacob looked like he'd seen a ghost from his past at her words.

"Oh, you remember me now," she sneered. "Yes, I'm the one you tried to pay off to leave your grandson alone. When that didn't work, you paid him off. It wasn't all Davis's fault. He'd been bought all of his life. He was weak. He gave in to the pressure you put on him. I would have been good for him, but you didn't think I was good enough for the likes of a Fallon. You paid him to abandon me and our child." A sob tore from her throat. "He refused to marry me. What was I supposed to do? I had no money. I couldn't support a child on my own. I had no choice. I had to kill my baby." Tears streamed down her face. There were horrified looks on their faces as she paced in front of them.

"Rich people can get away with anything while the rest of us are left to rot. Well, you're all gonna pay for what he did to me." She aimed the gun on Jacob.

The man on the floor moaned when he moved slightly. "Sue Ann, what's happening?" The gun wavered when she swung around to face him. "Why are you doing this?"

"Because of what he did to me." The gun turned back toward Jacob again. "You're all gonna pay."

For the last month, she had been ranting about 'what the Fallons did to her'. But she never explained. "Did you kill Kylie?" he asked. "What did she do to you?"

While she was distracted, Shep tried to get enough leverage against the wall to stand up. Even with his hands and feet bound, he might be able to knock her off balance enough that she'd drop the gun.

"Just because her father has money, she thought she was so much better than the rest of us. She tried to seduce my son."

"No, she didn't. Sam's…" A hacking cough stopped him from saying anything else for several seconds. "Sam's always been in love with Bailey," he finally finished.

"Then I should have killed them both. My son isn't gonna have anything to do with a Fallon."

"What are you talkin' about woman?" Seeing Shep move again, Elliott shifted to help cover the sound of his movement. "Her name's Baker, not Fallon."

"Are you as dumb as you look? Haven't you heard all the gossip? Don't you know who these people really are? His father was a Fallon." She pointed the gun at Ralph.

"So what?" He wanted to keep her talking. Giving up trying to stand, Shep was inching his way behind her. As long as she didn't notice, he might be able to knock her down without having to stand up.

"So what?" she shrieked. "The Fallons ruined my life. Haven't you been listening to me?" She pointed the gun at him again. "I shouldn't be married to a dumb ass like you. I'll take care of you after I rid the world of this family of vermin." She looked at each of them. "Who wants to go first?" The gun moved around the men on the floor. She'd save the old man for last. He would suffer the most watching his precious great-grandson die.

"What are you people doing on my land?" Roger Turner stepped over the threshold, surprising Sue Ann. "I told you not to come on my property without a search warrant," he stated indignantly. Swinging around at the sound of his voice, she automatically pulled the trigger. Roger dropped to the ground. Whether he was still breathing was anyone's guess.

There was a chorus of gasps behind their gags from the men on the floor. There was no telling who the unstable woman would shoot next.

Before she could pull the trigger again, a blur of tan and black fur leaped through the door knocking her to the side. She didn't drop the gun, and Gus's powerful jaws clamped down on her wrist.

With a scream of agony, she managed to keep holding onto the gun. Gus shook his head like he was holding a rag doll. There was no way she could aim at anyone, but she still managed to pull the trigger before dropping the gun to the ground.

Jacob screamed as he clutched at his shoulder, blood seeped between his fingers. "Jacob!" Victoria ran to his side while Jeremy tried to worm-crawl over to them.

"Get this beast off me," Sue Ann screamed. She thrashed around but couldn't dislodge the hundred-pound dog. His powerful jaws remained locked on her wrist.

Within minutes, the small shack was crowded with people. The sheriff entered first making sure the scene was secured before allowing Mona and Lena inside. While he cuffed Sue

Ann, they cut the ropes off the men.

Parker wasn't far behind in the big 4-wheeler. Sirens wailed in the distance. Not knowing what kind of carnage she would find she had called for an ambulance.

Mona went to check on Roger while Lena worked to set the men free. Feeling for a pulse, she shook her head at the sheriff's inquiring look. She guessed he had been dead before he hit the ground. Pulling off her jacket, she covered his face. Jose would have to figure out if there were any family members to notify.

Elliott Weston's wound wasn't life- threatening. He'd lost a lot of blood, but he would mend. Whether he would get back the half of his ranch he'd sold to Turner depended on how their partnership agreement had been written.

Kenneth was weak and his arms and shoulders were stiff from being forced behind his back for so long. But he was grateful to be able to move.

"How did you find us?" Once the sheriff had taken control of Sue Ann, Gus went to Shep lapping at his face. For his heroic efforts to save them, he got a good ear rub "She told us you'd found Kenneth," he explained. "She said he was in bad shape and couldn't be moved."

"She fed us the same line," Jacob said gruffly. "I should have known better than to believe her." The paramedic was working on his shoulder and he grimaced with pain.

After having only two small bottles of water a day, Kenneth was dehydrated. The paramedics wanted to take him to the hospital to be checked over. They had already put in an IV to administer fluids.

There wasn't room in the ambulance for all of them, and Jacob refused to go without Victoria and Jeremy. Parker wasn't sure of the reason behind his decision. He probably thought a country doctor wouldn't know what he was doing. She shook her head.

"I'll be out to take your statements," the sheriff said as Jacob and Victoria got into the 4-wheeler.

"The woman nearly killed us," Jacob snapped. "That's my statement." He had almost lost his great-grandson, not to mention his own life, but he still hadn't learned anything. Parker shook her head at him.

"As we learned a few years ago," Ben said when they were gathered in the great room at the ranch. "Revenge is a powerful emotion. Some people don't learn to let go of grudges until it's too late." Jacob's motives were a little more complicated. He had wanted something that didn't belong to him and was willing to do anything to get it. Ben wasn't sure whether the older man would ever learn that greed was a destructive emotion as well.

Bailey was sitting next to Jeremy, holding his hand. Occasionally Jacob would look at them with disapproval. She prayed that Jeremy was stronger than his father had been and wouldn't let Jacob buy him off. If that happened, he wasn't the man she thought he was.

CHAPTER TWENTY-ONE

It was another week before Jacob had an opportunity to talk to Jeremy alone. "Are you ready to come home now?"

"No, I'm not going back to Kansas. I've given you the opportunity to listen to my idea for personal wind turbines and manufacturing the components necessary to build them. You aren't interested. Kenneth is interested in helping me get it set up."

"What are you going to do for financing?"

Jeremy shrugged. "I think I have that covered as well." He wasn't going to tell his great-grandfather Parker and Shep were willing to help him out with the financing. Jacob already hated them. He wouldn't add fuel to that particular fire.

"I suppose your decision has something to do with that young woman."

"It does," Jeremy nodded. "But even if she wasn't in the picture, my answer would still be the same. I've tried to tell you I'm not cut out to be the CEO of Fallon Industries. It's too bad you refuse to listen."

He drew a deep breath. "After what just happened, I would think you would have learned that controlling someone else's life never works out. I can't say Sue Ann would have been good for my dad, but he should have been able to make that decision for himself."

Jacob waited for several beats before nodding his head. "All right. We can discuss this idea of yours when we get home. I just want you to come home."

"Bribery won't work either. I've made up my mind." He had approached Elliott Weston about buying the portion of his ranch Turner had bought. Weston jumped at the opportunity to be paid for the same piece of land twice. He wouldn't have a share in the enterprise Jeremy was planning, but that didn't matter to him.

Sam wanted what was left of his family's ranch. That was

okay with Jeremy. There was no reason a wind farm and a cattle ranch couldn't coexist.

Jeremy still didn't know how his dad had ruined Bill Hancock's life, but he wanted to make up for any past wrongs his dad and great-grandfather had committed. Since it was going to take a lot of work to implement his plan, he'd offered Mr. Hancock a job. Understandably, he'd been leery of the offer, but finally accepted.

Sue Ann was going to be in prison for the rest of her life. She had killed two people and kidnapped five others. Jeremy thought Elliot and Sam were better off without her. The baby she'd killed years ago was the one she was going to have with his father. Her remorse over the abortion had colored her thinking in everything she did.

~~~

"Are you goin' back to Kansas with your great-grandparents?" Bailey had never been timid before, but this man was very important to her.,

He nodded, a small grin lifting the corners of his lips. "Just long enough to sell my condo and pack up my things." He watched her face light up. "It seems I've acquired a house and a lot of land. I'm not a rancher, but I can learn as long as I have someone working beside me to show me the ropes."

"I'd like to apply for that job." She stood on tiptoes and kissed his chin.

"You're hired." He pulled her close, his lips closing over hers. He finally had a real family. He'd come to Texas looking for something undefinable. In Bailey, he had that. Jacob and Victoria would always be an important part of his life, but they were finally realizing they couldn't control him. Money wasn't the important thing in his life. It was too bad his dad hadn't learned that a long time ago. Maybe all of their lives would have been different.

ACKNOWLEDGMENTS

I praise God for the imagination He's given me, enabling me to write my books. I am so blessed by all He has given me. Without Him I can do nothing.

My thanks and gratitude also goes to Sandy Roedl, KaTie Jackson, Cece Blue, and Camala Klaus for their suggestions, editing and encouragement.

Ken Shriner, a retired Phoenix Police Detective was kind enough to answer my many questions regarding law enforcement. I'm grateful for his patience with me throughout the whole process. I've taken liberties with the way law enforcement works in an effort to move the story forward.

I'm most grateful to all of those who read my books. Thank you for your support and encouragement. I would enjoy hearing from you.

OTHER BOOKS BY SUZANNE FLOYD

Revenge Served Cold
Rosie's Revenge
A Game of Cat and Mouse
Man on the Run
Trapped in a Whirlwind
Smoke & Mirrors
Plenty of Guilt
Lost Memories
Something Shady
Rosie's Secret
Killer Instincts
Never Con A Con Man
The Games People Play
Family Secrets
Picture That
Trading Places
Chasing His Shadow
Rosie's Legacy
Drawing Conclusions
Rosie's Texas Family

Dear Reader:

Thank you for reading my book. I hope you enjoyed reading it as much as I did writing it. If you liked Rosie's Texas Family, I would appreciate it if you would tell your friends and relatives and/or write a review on Amazon. As an independent author, I don't have a publisher to promote my books. Reviews are the lifeblood of independent authors. I hope you will also check out my other books at Amazon.com.

Like me on Facebook at Suzanne Floyd Author or check out my web page at Suzanne Floyd.com.

Thank you,
Suzanne Floyd

P.S. If you find any errors, please let me know at: Suzanne.sfloyd@gmail.com. Before publishing, many people have read this book, but minds can play tricks by supplying words that are missing and correcting typos.

Thanks again for reading my book.

ABOUT THE AUTHOR

Suzanne is an internationally known author. She was born in Iowa, and moved to Arizona with her family when she was nine years old where she still lives in Phoenix with her husband, Paul. They have two wonderful daughters, two great sons-in-law and five of the best grandchildren around. Of course, she is just a little prejudiced.

Growing up and traveling with her parents, she entertained herself by making up stories. As an adult she tried writing, but family came first. After retiring in 2008, she decided it was her time. She still enjoys making up stories, and thanks to the internet she's able to put them online for others to enjoy.

When Suzanne isn't writing, she and her husband enjoy traveling around on their 2010 Honda Goldwing trike. She's always looking for new places to write about. There's a new mystery and a romance lurking out there to capture her attention.

Made in the USA
Las Vegas, NV
22 March 2023